Curfew

By

James Dean Perkins

ISBN: 0-7596-7009-9

This book is printed on acid free paper.

1stBooks – rev. 1/10/02

In Memory of Joshua Leigh Daniels
1984 - 2000

Had I been a faster writer,
would the ending have been different?

JDP

1

The townspeople of Crescent City had no idea what hit them. They couldn't even be sure when it all began. Peter Swann couldn't even be sure when it actually began. But for him, it started with the disappearance of little Mikey Miles.

Most of the accounts given here were researched afterwards. Many of the people involved were reluctant to be interviewed. Some of the people involved believe that just merely talking about it could start a chain reaction that would start another series of events. Others simply did not want to relive the nightmare. Obviously, some of the accounts are more of a speculative report, in nature.

This is how it began.

The quarter-moon played peek-a-boo behind the clouds as it shone through the window of Mikey's bedroom. But it wasn't the moon that kept Mikey awake that night.

Nor was it the silence that weighed so heavy in the air. Though the silence was so heavy that it was almost tangible.

Mikey had forgotten something outside. He had forgotten what it was that he had forgotten. Yet he knew there was something outside that needed his attention. Something was not right.

It had been four hours since his bedtime. he decided that he could wrestle with his memory no longer. He leaned out of his bed and felt around the floor until his fingers brushed against the crumpled heap that was his pants. With the logic of a four year old, he figured it would be a quick dash into the backyard and then back inside, so he skipped putting on shoes, a shirt, or a jacket.

The thick padding of the shag carpet concealed any noise his footsteps would have made. He made his way down the staircase. Just to be sure, he looked in at the floor of the living room. Nothing was there that needed his attention, as he knew would be the case. Next, he checked the kitchen, giving special attention under the kitchen table. Nothing. Whatever it was, it was outside. So he had made it all the way through the house, and out the kitchen door. His parents slept in sweet oblivion. They would never sleep so peacefully again.

As Mikey closed the door behind him, he realized his mistake. The northwestern wind was blowing its icy tendrils throughout the little harbor town. The ground was wet and so cold that it made his legs ache all the way up to his knees. The scimitar-shaped moon did little to dispel the darkness, nor did the streetlights which were too far away, and whose lights were filtered through too many redwood saplings.

At first glance, nothing seemed amiss. At second glance either. He padded his way out towards the center of the lawn. There was nothing laying on the lawn, no forgotten toy, no discarded clothing. Nothing was wrong, yet nothing seemed right.

He worked his way towards the far edge of the property. Perhaps he left something under the trees. It wasn't the trucks that he played with there. They could wait until morning. Mikey never brought them in.

His teeth were chattering. His pants were soaked halfway to his knees with freezing dew from the grass. His fingers were numb. The skin on his bare arms, chest, stomach, and back had reddened to the point that he was beginning to turn blue.

As he stood there contemplating his trucks, the cold air suddenly became more important than what he had forgotten. And the darkness began to take on an ominous atmosphere. For the first time since he was sent to his bed that night, Mikey sensed fear.

Every conversation Mikey had ever heard about the bogeyman came back to him. At four years old, there wasn't all that many, but at four years old the ones that took place were certainly enough. Yet there was something more terrifying than the bogeyman. There was something so horrible that the only people brave enough to talk about it was his parents. It was always dark outside when the conversation came up. And the description was apparently so abominable that only one word was needed to convey the message.

So there he was. He had forgotten his parents' warnings. His heart was pounding hard in his chest. He glanced around the yard. He had ventured too far from his house. Cold sweat trickled down his forehead.

Whatever it was that he had forgotten would have to wait until morning, when the sun was up. He would be dressed then, and it wouldn't be so cold. If he remembered what it was that he had forgotten, and if he still couldn't find it, he was sure that his mother could help him.

Then there was a noise. A noise that was not loud, yet Mikey heard it above the wind. It was a kind of hushing noise, like the kind his mom made when he was talking in church.

And then he heard the voices. They came from the dark area beneath the trees that provided the perimeter of his yard. There in the darkness where the moon and the streetlights could not penetrate, people spoke.

"There he is."

"What is he doing out here?"

"GET HIM!"

With arms and legs flailing, Mikey turned and ran towards the house. He didn't dare look back, but he could tell by the commotion from the bushes that they were hot on his pursuit. By the sounds that they made and the different directions the sounds were coming from Mikey Miles could tell that there was a lot of them.

At one moment, he tripped on the cuffs of his wet pants and landed face-down on the cold, wet grass. Fear forced him to his feet. He ran as fast as he could, but he didn't seem to be getting anywhere. He certainly wasn't getting anywhere, nearly fast enough.

He reached the back porch, finally. They hadn't caught him yet. He climbed the three steps on hands and knees. He was still free, but he could hear them. They were absolutely coming. He scampered to the door. With fingers that were trembling and stiff from the cold air and not at all coordinated in his state of panic, he tried to turn the doorknob. It wouldn't turn for him. He tried desperately with both hands, but the knob still held its place. He had locked himself out.

He felt a cold hand clamp down on his bare shoulder. It was colder than anything Mikey had ever felt before. It was colder than the north westerner that blew down from the arctic across the Pacific ocean and swept the little town nestled in the Redwoods. It was colder than the freezing dew that would cause a little barefooted boy's legs to ache all the way up to his knees. The fingers of this hand bit into Mikey's flesh, like an eagle's talons digging into its prey.

Mikey's heart was beating a tempo that threatened to be explosive. His throat felt as if it was pinched off. he was unable to pass air or sound. His stomach knotted. Somehow, he steeled his courage up enough to look down at the hand that had him pinned. The hand resembled a shadow, but it wasn't a play with lights. This hand was real. Slowly he brought his gaze up to the face of the person who belonged to the hand.

There it was at last. He had come face to face with that thing that so many people refuse to talk about. That thing that made grown men tremble and cry in the dark.

What was that word that his mother and father had used innumerable times to substitute the description of evil incomprehensible? What was that one word that he had forgotten? Just one word.

Curfew.

2

One of the blessings of living in a small town is that when tragedy strikes, the people pull together and act as one. What started as a parent's worst nightmare, at 7:30 that morning, turned into an anthill of commotion throughout the town. The whole community vowed to leave no stone unturned, no crawlspace unexplored, and no field untrampled, until little Mikey was back with his family. The Church of Jesus Christ of Latter Day Saints' Relief Society, a league of housewives, rallied together with a hearty banquet for those who were hard at work searching for the boy. When the Mormons had exhausted their supplies, The Seventh Day Adventists took over to supply dinner. The Jehovah's Witnesses made arrangements to have breakfast ready for the next morning, should the searching prove unsuccessful that day. All denominations performed their own prayer circles.

The search that started as an ever-widening circle, with the Miles' home as its epicenter, took on a new formation by 1:00 in the afternoon. Every man, woman, and child, twelve years and older, started at the south end of town and made a clean sweep to the north.

The Parks and Recreations Department scanned the marshes and the Redwoods. Cal-Trans ceased repairing roads and began searching sewers and drainpipes. The fishermen took the day off from trawling and crab pots. They used their boats to patrol the coastline. Every four-wheeler was utilized to search the rougher terrain.

The Police Department interrogated Mr. and Mrs. Miles for possible child-abuse. At that moment the man, who never raised his hand in anger to the boy, was their prime suspect. The Sheriff Department tactfully and discreetly interrogated every known sex offender and child molester in the area. The Highway Patrol sat up roadblocks just south of town on the 101, and again on the 101 at the Oregon border. They sat up another roadblock on the 199 just east of Hiouchi, where the South Fork road turns off. The town was completely sealed off.

The first day was a bust. Not one lead was found. It was as if little Mikey Miles had vanished into thin air.

Officer Alexandria Anita Martinez, or Marty if a person wanted her to answer, sat in the breakroom at headquarters. After her fourth cup of coffee, she felt no less tired. She felt bloated. Her lower intestines were cramping. She felt full. But the coffee did nothing to stave off her exhaustion.

Sergeant Theodore Jones, her senior partner, was sorting through a box of doughnuts that sat on the conference-size table. When he failed to find a doughnut that appealed to him, he pushed the box away.

"Cops and doughnuts. I'm so tired of that cliché. Oh, wait. There's one."

He reached his hand into the box and pulled a cinnamon swirl out of the box. He took three healthy bites and a large swig of coffee, sat back, and smiled. Jones was missing his molars, so he loved to mix his chips with soda, cookies with milk, and doughnuts with coffee. He would swish the liquids around in his mouth until the solids were thoroughly soaked. Then he would gum the food a few times with the section of his mouth where the molars used to be. And then he would let the whole mouthful slide down his throat.

Marty never said as much, but it nauseated her to watch her partner eat. As much as she tried to ignore the whole ordeal, her eyes were fixed in morbid curiosity. She contemplated grabbing a doughnut for herself. Usually, she avoided sweets and junk food, but a sugar high could be useful at a time like this.

She had a doughnut in her hand and was scrutinizing the sticky, goopey sugar-slime that coated the deep-fried ball of yeast. If she ignored the calorie count that would put her daily allowance through the roof, she still had to contend with the artery-blocking cholesterol. If she relinquished then, what would she have to do to erase its affects from her system? And more importantly, what would restrain her the next time a doughnut was placed before her? Plus, there was the fact that the doughnut didn't appeal to her, at all. She was about to put the sticky mess back in the box when the captain came in.

"Jones, Martinez. Good, I found you. I need you to take off. You'll be covering the overnights, tonight. You guys have any problems with that?"

"Nope." Jones spoke around a mouthful of doughnuts and coffee. Some of the coffee seeped out the corner of his mouth. He wiped it away with his thumb.

"No Captain."

"There's gonna be a couple of experts coming up from Eureka in the morning. They should be here in time to hook up with you before the end of your shift. Give them a run-down on the Mikey Miles case. There's a folder on my desk. Jones, you can't miss it. Make sure they get it. Any questions?"

"Nope."

"No Captain."

"Go home and get some rest. And Martinez, that especially means you."

"Yes Captain."

The Captain did a stiff about-face out of the breakroom. Marty stood up to leave. Jones was still enjoying his doughnut.

"Hey Marty are you going to eat that?" Jones pointed a finger at the unscathed pastry.

Marty glanced back at the blob of carbohydrates and preservatives. "No, no. You have it."

"I wasn't... I just thought it shouldn't... Okay, I'll eat it on the way home." Jones reached across the table and snatched up the doughnut, in case Marty were to have a change of heart. He added sheepishly, "Amy won't know I'm coming. This will hold me over until dinner."

Marty had already left the room.

Marty tossed around in her bed. The four cups of coffee that didn't keep her alert earlier was now keeping her from sleeping. she sat up in bed. She never could sleep while the sun was up.

Reluctantly, she arose. Donning her workout clothes, she went into the living room. Between two dining room chairs, she executed twenty-four dips, three more than the day before yesterday. Without a break, she went into her push-ups. Then hooking her toes under the couch, she put herself through the ordeal of sit-ups and a series of crunches. In the center of the living room, she did her hamstring lifts and tush-tucks.

She had manage to work up a sweat, but standing in the bathroom door and staring at the shower, she realized that she still wasn't tired. She thought of her aerobics videos. It just didn't feel like it would be enough. She eyed the front door.

The Captain wanted her to get rest. What awaited on the other side of the door was a direct violation to the Captain's request. One look in the full-length mirror, and the decision was made. She refused to allow herself to be slothful, regardless of whoever made the request. She took off for the beach. It was a little over a mile to the beach. If the tide was out, there was a stretch of shoreline on the south end of town that a person could jog for a mile and a half or more. If the tide was in, one could still jog along the 101. She was in luck. Though it was hard on shoes to have to dodge the surf, she preferred the sand over pavement. Sand offered less impact and greater aerobics.

Upon arriving home, she showered, threw on a t-shirt, climbed into her panties, and curled up in bed with a Danielle Steele novel. She was asleep before she finished reading the first page.

For Jones, it was easier to find sleep. He had finished the doughnut before he had reached the first stoplight. By the time he turned his dodge caravan into the driveway, his eyes were half closed.

"You're home. Did you find him?" His wife sat down at the dining room table opposite her husband.

"No, but we will."

"Do you want coffee?"

"Naw, I got to go back in tonight."

"Oh honey, I hate it when you work the overnights."

"Someone's got to do it. We're doubling up until the boy's found."

"Such an awful thing to happen. Such a God-awful thing."

"It happens."

"But not here. Not in Crescent City."

"It happens anywhere."

"Such a shame. His poor mother must be a nervous wreck. A God-awful nervous wreck."

"Yeah, she's a wreck." He could tell by the quiver in her voice that she was on the verge of tears. "They got some hotshots coming up from Eureka, tomorrow morning. We're going to find the kid."

"Why don't you go lie down? I'll wake you up when dinner is ready."

"I'm not really hungry. Could you make me a ham sandwich? We got any of those pickle slices left? Lettuce. Tomatoes. Cheese, the white stuff."

"Why don't I make dinner?" She said, slightly exasperated.

He chuckled. "I'd really rather have a ham sandwich." He stood up, retrieved a beer from the fridge, and headed off for the living room. "Mustard, but not a whole lot, just on the one side. Potato chips. You know how I like potato chips — inside the sandwich."

He settled into his recliner, turned on the local news, drained the can of beer, and slipped off into tranquillity. Amy came in to check on him. Satisfied that he was asleep, she returned to the kitchen where she wrapped the ham sandwich and tucked it into his lunchpail, along with a thermos of kool-aid, string cheese, an apple, and a bag of chips. She returned to the living room, pulled out an afghan from the hall closet. She took great care to gently spread the afghan over her napping husband. Then she located the wind-up alarm clock, sat the alarm for 10:00, and sat it on the stand next to his recliner. When that was done, she headed off to the bedroom so that she could take a nap also.

"What a God-awful shame." She said, as she laid her head on her pillow.

Peter Swann sat behind his desk. It was always upsetting to hear about a child being taken from his or her home. He had been successful in returning several children to their families. All to often, their abductors were usually an estranged parent, a relative, or a baby-sitter who, for one reason or another, felt the child would be better off away from their natural parents. Yet, more and more each year, children were vanishing without a trace, world wide. Peter had a file cabinet full of unsolved cases. He had a feeling that little Mikey Miles would be another.

Clark Williams, his partner and best friend for more years than he could remember, came over and plopped himself down on Peter's desk. Peter grabbed his Styrofoam coffee cup to keep it from getting knocked over. As an afterthought, he drank the last of its contents.

"Hey, Pete. Do you think you could pile a little bit more of your paperwork here, so it'll be a little more comfortable for me to sit down?"

"No."

"Are you ready for this trip tomorrow?"

"No." Peter responded, but then he added, "What the heck, they'll probably have him found by the time we get there."

"I'm sure they will. What time do you want to head out?"

"We better leave by five. I'll call Crescent City before we go."

"You ever been to Crescent City? They have some great seafood restaurants up there."

"Yeah, several times. It's a nice little town."

"Okay, I'll see you at five." Clark grabbed the Styrofoam cup and placed it upside down on the sheet of paper that Peter had been working on.

"What did you do that for?"

"Don't worry. It was empty."

"It's still going to leave a ring."

"Pete, buddy. I've been meaning to talk to you. You've got this perfectionist thing going. It's very unattractive, and it makes everybody have to work that much harder."

"You are a scab. That's all you have ever been. That's all you'll ever be. You're a loser. You will never amount to anything."

"Thanks, Mom. I'll see you at five." Clark stood up and started to walk away, but then he turned around again. "Pete, buddy, get some rest. It's going to be a long day."

"I will. You too."

Peter watched his partner and best friend walk away. He chewed on the end of his pen and thought of a little boy named Mikey. He knew he wouldn't get much rest that night.

Dread had failed to leave him.

3

The patrol car made a second pass at Mikey's pre-school. It was a longshot, but longshots were all that was left. Conversations were at a minimum. Marty found that after eight months of being teamed up with Jones, they still had very little in common. On the days that the police force was at a minimum, Marty drove her own squad car. She appreciated the solitude, on those days.

Jones turned the car west on Washington and headed towards the ocean. They planned on making a sweep by the airport. If nothing surfaced at the airport, they would drive up to Point St. George and do a foot search of the area. Point St. George had several trails and tide pools that naturally attracted kids of all ages. It was unfathomable that a four year old boy would make it all the way out there by himself. Another longshot.

Marty could tell by Jones' expression that he was just as heartbroken as she was that the Miles' boy wasn't found while they were sleeping. She didn't dislike Jones. He had a big heart and genuinely cared for the people in this area.

In a tight knit community such as Crescent City, everybody knew everyone else. If they didn't, they were usually close to someone who did. The Jones and the Miles belonged to the same congregation. Marty's dad had been Robert Miles Little League coach. Sarah Miles was only two grades ahead of Marty in high school.

Marty had never met Mikey Miles, but she was well aware of what he looked like. His picture was plastered on posters throughout the town. The local office supply store volunteered to print copies, and the townsfolk rallied to post Mikey's picture on every shop window, on every telephone pole, and on every street sign. Friends and family members posted signs as far away as Brookings, Medford and Eureka. The same picture was faxed to every law enforcement agency between Portland and San Francisco, and as far east as Salt Lake City. More than a few residents scanned the picture into their computers and placed it on the Internet.

They were about a mile from the airport when a call came in over the police band. The message was for them to waste no time getting back to the station. Jones flipped on the lights, but he left the siren off. He pushed the speed of the cruiser up to a pace that he still felt safe with. At the turn off for the airport, the cruiser turned left, instead of right, and followed the coastline back towards town.

When they pulled up before the station, the night duty officer was standing in front with Robert Miles.

"She's gone." Robert announced to the two officers as they were exiting their vehicle.

"What?" Marty gasped.

"The doctor gave her some sedatives. I thought she went to bed. But then she came out of the bedroom all dressed. She said she could her his voice calling for her. And then she ran outside. She's gone."

Marty was the first to speak up. "Do you know which way she went?"

"No." There was panic in his voice. "But she might have gone to Endert's park. They like to hang out there together."

"Sit tight, Robert. We'll check it out." Jones called out as he turned and ran back to the driver's side. Marty hopped in beside him. Seconds later, the cruiser was screaming away into the night.

Peter Swann had set his clock-radio for 3:00 A. He sat his battery-powered travel clock for 3:00, with the red dot lit up on AM, just in case the electricity went out and the clock-radio didn't go off. And then, knowing how unreliable batteries could be, he sat his wind-up clock by the battery-powered clock. He adjusted the little red hand so that it pointed directly at the three.

He packed two overnight bags and placed them on the back seat of his Gold-colored Cimmeron Cadillac. Standing with the back door open, he stared at the luggage. If he needed more, he could always do laundry at the coin-op or purchase another outfit. God-willing, they wouldn't have to spend more than a day in Crescent City.

In the living room, he scanned the area that would need attention, in case he was stuck in Crescent City for any length of time. He checked all of the recent mail for any bills he might have over-looked. When he was satisfied with that, he moved on to the kitchen. When he had finished searching the fridge and the shelves for time-sensitive perishable, he double-checked the three clocks.

After all that, Peter was awake by 2:55. He was shaved, showered, and dressed by 3:45. When 4:15 came around, he was already sitting at his desk in the Detective Division. He thought about calling Clark to see if he was awake. He picked up the phone and called the Crescent City Police Department, instead.

When he hung up, he ran out of the office building, jumped into the gold-colored Cadillac, and pointed it towards Clark's place. Clark had just stepped out of his house and was walking towards his own car, when Peter pulled up.

"What are you doing here? I was coming to the Office." Clark tossed his overnight bags in the back seat, and climbed into Peter's Cadillac.

"We have to leave now."

"Why? What happened?"

"The boy's mother is missing."

"Oh, wow!"

A quick drive-by revealed nothing. They followed the road towards the beach. Marty operated the searchlight, while Jones maneuvered the vehicle. Occasionally, a tree, a maintenance building, or a set of lavatories would obscure their view. But for the most part, there was nothing to see. The park was deserted.

The car swung up around the water-treatment plant and down the road the led to the fisherman's dock. When they reached the dock, Jones spun the cruiser around, so it pointed back towards town. They exited the vehicle and did a foot search of the dock.

The sky was uncommonly clear for this time of the year. The moon was nearly invisible, except for the ring of light around its edge. Tomorrow night, there would be no moon at all. The foghorn, that stood sentry at the end of the Jetty, boomed out its wailful warning in a metronomic syntony. A bank of fog was sitting on the water, two miles offshore.

"What's that?" Jones stopped along the dock and turned his attention back across the harbor, towards the park.

"What?" Marty froze in her tracks. The foghorn blared its resonance.

"I thought I heard something."

Marty listened to the intermittent silence. The foghorn droned.

Waves lapped at the dock's pilons. Nothing.

"There! Come on. Let's go." Jones took off towards the car.

Marty still hadn't heard anything but the foghorn and waves. She thought of asking her partner for a more descriptive explanation, yet she trusted her partner's instinct. For someone who never worked out, Jones managed to get a good lead on her.

The gold-colored Cadillac had left the coastline, as the 101 turned in-land to clip a pit-stop in half. People called the pit-stop Orick, California. If not for a mini-market, a church, a school, a tavern, and five tourist shops that specialized in redwood carvings and redwood burls, the town of Orick would have been nothing but a glen populated by Roosevelt elks.

Peter had always wanted to stop and check out the shops in Orick. He admired the carvings sitting on the roadside. There just never seemed to be the time. "Someday." He thought to himself. He imagined what it would be like to have an eight foot tall grizzly bear, carved out of driftwood, sitting in his living room.

"What the...!" Peter swerved and then re-compensated.

"What?"

"You didn't see him?"

"No. See who?"

"That idiot. He was standing right in the road.

Clark laughed.

"I'm not kidding! Man! Climb out and see if he carved his initials on the roof." Peter showed no sign of slowing down.

Clark laughed harder.

"I'm not kidding! He has to be missing some toes."

Clark tried to choke back the laughter, but that made his chest hurt.

"Jesus! Should we go back and check on him?"

"Hey, no way." Clark blurted out between snorts. "I've seen that movie."

"What movie?"

"You know, the woman hits the hitchhiker with her car. Next thing you know, the hitchhiker's bloody hand is crawling over the grill."

"Man! This is not the time."

"Are you sure there was somebody? It's pretty dark out there."

"All right. That's it. I'm turning around."

"No, no. You're right. We don't have time."

"You should've seen his face."

"Why? Did you?"

"No. But if you had, you wouldn't be laughing now."

Clark caught a glimpse of his partner's ashen face, lit by the dashboard lights. He started laughing again.

"I can see the job interview now. 'I used to be a police detective.' 'What happened?' 'I drove over the top of a transient.'"

Clark's eyes watered. He laughed so hard that he thought he was going to die.

Tires screamed, as the squad car skidded to a stop. They jumped out. Jones left the engine running. He ran around the front of the car.

"This way!" He called out.

Marty was close behind. She could here the voice for herself, now. It struck her as odd that Jones could have heard the voice all the way back at the dock. Her ears were still ringing from the droning foghorn.

"I hear you, honey. Mommy's here. Mommy's coming. I hear you."

They were running on a footpath that divided the property of the water-treatment plant from the beach. When they reached the end of the trail, they were back on the road that circumferenced the park. At first, there was no sign of the owner of the voice.

"There!" Marty shouted. She pointed towards the soccer field. Though the view was greatly obscured by a row of coniferous trees, there was a lone figure in the middle of the field. Sarah Miles was running haphazardly.

Jones grabbed Marty by the shoulders. "Get the car!" He shouted. He took off across the road, towards the field.

Marty reached the car, climbed in behind the wheel, and instinctively reached for the mike. "We found her! We're down at the soccer field at Endert's. Send backup!" She put the car in gear.

"Look! There he is again!" Clark said referring to a lone, dark figure sitting along the side of the road. The area was lit up by the sodium lights, in the parking lot of the Trees of Mystery. But the lights did nothing to reveal any detail of the strange, dark figure.

"This is getting old."

"I'm just saying..."

"Do you honestly believe that that's the same person we've passed twice before?"

"It's kind of hard to say. I mean, I don't know what I would do if some police detective tried to run me over."

"It's getting old." Peter spoke to the window on the driver's side door.

"What?"

"Check reality, Clark. Check reality."

Oddly enough, it was too early in the season for travelers. And it was too cold for transients. The 101 was definitely more populated than usual.

Marty exited the vehicle and strode across the field. She had an eerie feeling that something was wrong. Sarah Miles was no longer running. She was crouched on the ground, trembling. It was the classic defensive position against attack. As Marty closed the distance between the Miles woman and herself, she could hear Sarah sobbing. Jones was nowhere to be seen. It was as if he had vanished without a trace.

Marty could hear the sirens of her backup approaching, from the distance. The foghorn moaned.

4

The gold-colored cadillac pulled up in front of the police station, at 6:15. The sky in the eastern horizon had brightened just barely enough to show the silhouettes of the tree-lined mountains. Very little movement was going on. Most of the town was still asleep.

Peter climbed out of the car, stretched, and took a couple of deep, cleansing breaths. There was an edge of frost in the air. He could hear Sea lions barking, down at the harbor. Somewhere further off, a foghorn was moaning.

Peter was taken back by the beauty and simplicity of this small town. It was not his first time visiting Crescent City, yet each time he came, this quaint little village enchanted him. Small towns always fascinated him.

He started to walk towards the station, but then he realized that he was alone. He turned back towards the car. Clark had not moved. At first, he thought Clark had dozed off, but as he approached the car he noticed that Clark's eyes were open. He was just sitting there, staring. Peter rapped on the window.

Slowly, Clark diverted his attention from the windshield to the side window. his eyes focused on Peter. He opened the door and lacksidaisically climbed out.

"Are you okay?"

"I'm fine. I just wanted to make sure the car was completely stopped. I don't need any detective driving over the top of me."

"That's not funny."

"I'm just saying..."

"It's getting old."

The lobby was incredibly small. A few short strides from the front door brought them face to face with a security glass, with a combination microphone/speaker drill into it. On the other side of the window, there sat a young uniformed officer. Peter introduced himself and then Clark. He stated their purpose. The caged officer seemed uncertain of his next course of action, so he motioned for the detectives to have a seat. After several minutes had passed, the officer picked up the receiver to the phone located in front of him and began pushing buttons. When he finally replaced the receiver, he leaned into the mike.

"Excuse me, sirs. Hello. Excuse me."

Clark had found an interesting article in an outdated Popular Mechanics. Peter had occupied himself with the various plaques that were hanging against the dark wood paneled wall.

"Hello?"

It took a moment for the detectives to realize that the officer was addressing them. They approached the window.

"The Captain will see you now."

Clark reached for the heavy, plated door first. The door wouldn't budge. He let go of the door knob just as the officer behind the desk pressed the buzzer. Clark grabbed the door knob again, but the officer had already released the buzzer. Clark turned around and glared at the young man behind the window.

"Quit it." Peter poked Clark in the shoulder. Peter grabbed the door knob and waited for the officer to press the buzzer, again.

"Sorry," The officer said apologetically. "It's kind of tricky."

Clark shook his head in disgust, as he followed his partner through the doorway. "You know that wasn't my fault, right?"

The Captain was standing on the other side of the door, in what turned out to be a short and narrow part of an L-shaped hallway. He was shorter than either had expected. he stood about 5'7". His reddish-blonde hair was cropped short, a high and tight. His uniform was pressed and starched. Each crease stood out in a perfect, unbroken line. Each button was polished. Peter knew, without looking, that if he were to glance down he would see his reflection in the Captain's spit-shined shoes.

"My name is Captain Stockton. And you are Detective Swann."

Peter raised his hand to acknowledge his name, and then shook hands with the Captain.

"And you must be Detective Williams."

"Yes, sir." Clark shook his hand.

"If you boys will follow me, I'll take you somewhere where we can talk."

The Captain led them into a conference room, just a few paces beyond the lobby door. The room was immensely larger than the lobby. It was furnished with a large table, with several padded chairs positioned around it.

Peter and Clark took their seats closest to the head of the table. The Captain remained standing at the head of the table. He pulled two manila envelopes out of a folder and handed one to each of the detectives.

"This is the file on the Mikey Miles case. There has been some developments not reflected in the file. Apparently, in a moment of distress, his mother ran out looking for him. We sent a couple of our officers out to find her. When they did, she was running around the park, calling to her son. The two officers were separated when the junior officer went to retrieve their vehicle. When she returned, the mother was still there, but the other officer was missing." Captain Stockton looked up at the clock above the door and then down at his own watch. "That was about an hour and a half ago."

"Has the Bureau been notified?" Clark asked.

"They have. It's still too early to be alarmed, but they're sending a team to assist with this case. They'll be flying out of San Francisco tomorrow morning."

"Did the Miles woman give any explanation to the officer's whereabouts?" It was Peter's turn to speak.

"When Officer Martinez returned, Mrs. Miles was rambling incoherently. She's been taken to the E.R.. The doctor has her heavily sedated."

"And this Officer Martinez stated that she didn't see anything?" Peter continued.

"That's correct. I've known Marty since she was a little girl. She's very factual." Captain Stockton paused thoughtfully. "Now you know about as much to this case as I do. Where would you like to begin?"

"Is Martinez up to answering questions?" Peter asked as he stood up.

"Certainly. If you will follow me." The Captain led them down the hallway to the breakroom. Marty was sitting at the table. She appeared to be incredibly poised, considering what had just happened.

After a brief interrogation, Clark found himself being annoyed with Marty. She seemed to be lacking any emotions. He was stirred by her beauty. Beyond her police uniformity, she had a pixie-like charm. But her absence of emotion towards the disappearance of her partner disturbed him.

"Tell me one more time, why were you and your partner separated?"

"We were on foot. We found Sarah Miles. Jones sent me back for the car. He continued on towards the woman, on foot."

"Why do you suppose he sent you back for the car, rather than doing it himself?"

"I can only speculate, but I am a faster runner than Jones. The Joneses and the Miles attend the same church. They're good friends."

"How fast can you run the mile?"

"Six, nineteen. Recorded."

"Wow, not bad." Clark paused and pretended to go over his notes. His fastest time for the mile was probably closer to seven minutes. He preferred to run for distance, rather than for speed. "Okay, so how fast can Jones run the mile?"

"I don't know if he can even run a mile."

Clark pretended to rub the spot between his eyebrows with the tip of his middle finger. In actuality, he was trying to disguise his smirk. "Okay, so you retrieved the car. What happened next?"

"She was kneeling on her hands and knees. He was gone."

Clark searched her face for any sign of emotion. He found none. "What was she doing?"

"Excuse me?"

"Was she praying? Was she looking for something?"

"Cowering."

"I'm sorry. Could you say that again?"

"She was cowering, Sir."

"From who? Jones?"

"Not likely."

"From who then? You?"

"No. I don't know who or what she was cowering from?"

"What makes you think that she was cowering?"

"She was scared. When I saw her the first time, she was running around calling for her son. She was hopeful. But when I saw her the second time, she was scared."

"But you weren't there when Jones reached her. Your partner could've ran up on the woman, smacked her around a couple of times, and ran off for the beach or town. Right?"

"Why would he?"

"Suppose you tell me."

"I wouldn't know." Marty's frustration for the Detective was becoming more obvious.

"Did she have anything to say about your partner's disappearance?"

"Yes, but it didn't make any sense. She said that first he was there. And then they were there with him. And then they were there, but he wasn't. And then they weren't there anymore."

"They who?"

"She didn't know."

"What did they look like?"

"She didn't know."

"I don't get it."

"Neither does anyone else."

Clark rubbed his forehead again, this time out of frustration. He turned to Peter, who up to this point has been uncharacteristically quiet. "Peter, do you have any questions?"

"Just one. I understand they call you 'Marty'." He waited for her to nod. "Marty, you've been working all night. How would you like to be excused?"

Marty was expecting another barrage of questions from Peter. She paused before answering. "Yes, please."

Peter motioned towards the door.

"Sir, before I go. I would like to be a part of the investigation."

"I'll bet you would." Clark said.

Peter scowled briefly at Clark. "Well actually, Marty, tomorrow morning, it all gets turned over to the bureau. But we have it until then. Go get some rest."

"Thank you." Marty stood up and left.

Once she had closed the door behind her, Clark turned to Peter. What's next, Boss?"

"Let's go check on the Miles woman."

"Hey, Pete. How fast can you run the mile."

"My fastest time was five, twenty-three. But that was a hundred years ago."

"A hundred years?"

"Yeah, give or take eighty-five years."

Clark nodded his head in acknowledgment. "Boy, if you seen it once, you've seen it a million times." He stood up to leave. "A junior partner develops a hatred for her senior partner and has him done away with."

Peter did a double-take. "You've never felt that way, have you?"

"No."

"I'm not kidding, now. Have you ever felt that way?"

"No. But I'm never going to stand in front of the car while you're starting it."

"Give it a rest, Mister. Just give it a rest."

Unfortunately for the city, There wasn't a Psych ward in the hospital. Any patient needing psychiatric attention was held in a little room, only slightly larger than a walk-in closet. The little room was equipped with a cot that was bolted down to the floor. The room had one heavy door that was locked from the outside and a shatter-proof window for observation.

Peter and Clark could see for themselves that they weren't going to be able to interview Sarah Miles. She was going through fits of laughing hysterically and sobbing uncontrollably. Her doctor approached the two detectives. He was a kind, gentle-faced man. His hair was dark and just long enough to be considered unkempt. His salt-and-peppered beard betrayed his true age. He was tall and portly and spoke with a drawl.

"She hasn't spoken a word since she arrived. I've given her diazepam to help calm her, but it doesn't seem to be taking hold. As you can see, she just sits there on the bed. She becomes terrified anytime anyone enters the room. When she first arrived, she paced, but..."

"But what?" Peter was studying the Miles woman.

"Well, it's odd. I mean, I've heard the expression, but I've never actually seen it with my own eyes."

"Seen what? Doctor?" Clark prodded.

"Well, she is quite literally afraid of her own shadow."

They stood there, watching the woman.

"Do you have any more questions for me?"

"No. Wait. One more question, Doc. What would cause her to be like this?"

"Trauma. Fear. Intense fear."

5

2:55 am. Five minutes to three. Five minutes to lunch. Alex Alden glanced down at the brown paper sack. Peanut butter sandwiches again. He's been married for over three years, now, and he's been working for Scud Security, Inc. for a little over a year and a half. Each night, it was peanut butter sandwiches.

He didn't mean to rag on his wife. She was the greatest. She was a great cook and a great conversationalist. She went through great pains to accommodate his little quirks. When he got home, she was ready to romp in the blankets if he was in the mood. She was ready to cuddle up beside him and sleep, if he wasn't in the mood for romping. Sex with her was good. The honeymoon wasn't over yet, nor would it ever be if Alex had anything to say about it. Yes indeed, he had the greatest wife in the whole world. She was the best friend he had ever had. There wasn't anything he would change — except for the peanut butter sandwiches.

Three minutes to go. Alex's bank was three blocks down and three blocks over. If Alex cut across the parking lots and utilize the alleys, he was sure he could get to the ATM, check his balance, backtrack to the office and cross the street to Safeway before his lunch hour was up.

Two minutes to go. Alex was up and moving towards the door. He discarded the brown sack and its contents into a waste paper receptacle. He clocked out at 02:59 and stepped out into the night.

The same wind that brings in the fog and the rain had scrubbed the sky clean of all clouds. With no clouds in the sky, there was nothing to trap the sun's heat and hold in reserve for the night. Alex Alden zipped up his jacket.

Scud Security, Inc. was located in a strip mall, on a mile stretch where the 101 splits as it flows through town. If Alex crossed the northbound lanes, it would take him right into the parking lot of Safeway. But he wanted to check the balance on his ATM card first, so he headed west, across the southbound.

He didn't bother to cross at the light, nor did he bother to check for traffic. At this time of night, the town was dead. A half of a block over and a half a block down, Alex cut through a parking lot. Something was wrong. He felt as if he was being watched.

He scanned the area. There was a telephone booth off in the distance. He couldn't be sure if it was a play with the lights, but there appeared to be a man standing in the booth.

He crossed an intersection to the far corner and through another parking lot. The town clock showed that only five minutes had elapsed. He still had plenty of time.

On the other side of the parking lot was an area the kids called the skateboard maze. It consisted of a labyrinth of steps and ramps. It made a great arena for skateboarding and rollerblading. It was also a perfect hideout for illegal drinking and illicit drugs.

Alex was halfway through the area when he noticed a couple across the way and off to his left. They seemed to be involved in an intimate conversation, judging by how close they were standing to each other. It was hard to determine where one person ended and the other began. They stopped talking to turn and look at him. It was odd that he couldn't see their faces, but they were standing in the shadows. That would explain it.

"It's way too late for kids to be out." He said out loud to himself. He glanced down at his watch and pressed on towards the bank.

On the other side of the maze was an alley that ran between two shops. When he had executed the alley, he froze in his tracks. There was that feeling again. The hairs on the back of his neck stood on ends. Someone was there.

The streetlights in this area seemed dimmer than normal. Across the street in a little shop sat up as a karate mojo, a silhouette stood watching. Alex felt his heart skip a beat. He wasn't certain if it was an actual person or a poster. It might even be a dummy. Alex had never enrolled in any karate courses. He couldn't be certain what one would find in a karate mojo.

He collected his wits and headed off across the street. He made a point of looking out of the corner of his eyes. The figure was definitely moving. And what was even more unnerving, the figure was watching him.

Alex quickly dashed across the street. After transversing another parking lot, and another alley, he found himself standing in front of the bank. The ATM was just around the corner.

Maybe it was out of fear, or maybe it was just out of habit, whatever the cause was, Alex pulled out three hundred dollars, instead of the twenty he had originally planned on grabbing. He paused for a moment to contemplate his avenue back to the office. As he stuffed the bills into his wallet, along with his ATM card, he decided to take the same route. After all, he was a grown man, and he was just being silly.

The moment he exited the alley and entered the parking lot for the karate mojo, he heard a strange voice call his name. He turned to see who it was. Three dark figures stood at the other end of the alley.

"We've come to get you." The voice continued.

"No!" He cried out in a high pitched squeal that, under other circumstances, would have been embarrassing.

He darted across the parking lot. Suddenly, three more dark figures stood up from behind bushes that grew along the sidewalk. He was trapped.

Before he had a chance to decide his next move, Alex felt an icy cold press against his back. It seemed to be penetrating him. He wondered how his wife would react to this news. He thought about those peanut butter sandwiches. They really weren't all that bad.

The plane made its final approach into the Eureka-Arcata airport. It had been a rocky flight from San Francisco. Special Agent Willard preferred to fly at night, so he could sleep through the flight. But this time sleep escaped him.

He watched the young stewardess, as she approached the group of four men. She was in her early thirties. Her hair was a dark chestnut color that, he was pretty sure, came from a bottle. She wore slacks instead of a skirt, and her jacket revealed nothing. But her smile could melt ice cubes, or so he thought to himself.

"Isn't it amazing what a smile can do?" He said to Special Agent Baker, who sat directly across the aisle from him.

"Tell me about it." Baker said in return.

The plane lurched, and the stewardess had to grab the backs of a couple of seats to keep from falling. The smile completely disappeared, if only for a moment. When she had regained her composure and her smile, she continued walking towards the FBI agents. She bent over at the hips so her face was level with theirs.

"The airport is closed, but your plane will be waiting to take you to Crescent City."

"Which gate will that be?" Special Agent Willard noticed that she had large, beautiful eyes, but he found himself staring at her lips as she spoke. His imagination was taking off in fleets of fancies. Each brief fantasy began with him grabbing her by her shoulders, pulling her down on his lap, and kissing those lips.

She giggled. "Arcata only has two gates. Your plane will be parked directly ahead of this one. You'll see." She stood up and walked towards the front of the plane. Willard and Baker carefully scrutinized her posterior.

"I could do that." Willard put emphasis on each word.

"What about your old lady?"

"Well, it's like this. Eventually, I'm sure I could forgive myself for cheating on my wife. But if I had a chance to sleep with that, and I didn't jump on it... I can't think of any man that could forgive himself."

"So relax. You don't have a chance."

"Shut up. You're ruining this for me."

When the stewardess had made her way to the front of the plane, she grabbed the mouthpiece to the intercom. "Ladies and gentlemen, we are on our final approach to Arcata. The captain has turned on the no smoking sign and the seat belt sign. Please return all tables and seats to their upright position. And thank you for flying with us."

"Better wake up Sutton." Willard motioned to the window seat beside Baker.

"At least one of us was able to sleep." Baker gave Sutton a nudge.

"Yeah, as a matter of fact, we should have him work the case while we catch up on our sleep."

"Yeah, right." Baker snorted.

The landing was rougher than Willard would have preferred. But then again, aren't they all? Willard thought to himself. When they had grabbed their baggage out of the overhead compartments and struggled towards the exit, they were surprised to see just how small the airport actually was. When Pierce stepped out onto the stairs, he made a comment that implied that someone could steal the building on a flatbed semi.

The stewardess heard the comment and quipped, "Don't make fun of our airport, Mister. After all, you're going to Crescent City."

"Is Crescent City's airport smaller than this one?" Pierce asked, with more than a little astonishment.

"You'll see. That's your plane over there." She said pointing towards a twelve-seater.

With bags in tote, they meandered their way over to the small airplane that was going to take them on the last leg of their journey. They climbed the portable steps and was greeted by another stewardess. Though she was approximately the same age as the last, and she was attractive enough for all normal purposes, Willard just didn't feel anything for her. It was the smile. This one was too professional, too forced.

Each seat was a window seat. Since there was just the four of them traveling, there was no seating assignments. However, the all too professional stewardess asked that they all sit behind the wings. "Just until we're airborne." She added.

"I wonder if we have to move to the nose of the plane, when it's time to land. You know, to get the plane pointed in the right direction." Pierce said to the other three.

"Better be careful, Pierce. Or they'll have us flapping the wings. Stroke. Stroke. Stroke." Sutton returned.

"This is the Captain speaking," Pierce said in a mocked intercom voice. "We need everybody to move to the right side of the plane now. We're banking."

Willard turned his attention to the activities outside the plane. From his view through the porthole-sized window, he could see people bustling. He counted at least three people loading the rest of their baggage, fueling, and checking the plane. But then, out by the tree line, he saw two other figures approaching the plane. How sad, he thought, the pilots have to resort to using the bushes as an outhouse.

The two people from the bushes entered the plane. They paused long enough to turn their attention to the four passengers, and then stepped into the cockpit.

"That's odd."

"What's that?"   Baker was hoping for any kind of conversation that didn't involve rowing ships, whips and tom-toms.

"Well, when those guys stepped on to the plane, I couldn't make out any features. It's as if they were shadows."

"The lighting is bad."

The pilots stepped aboard the plane and went straight to the cockpit. Willard waited to see if the first two were going to leave. In a few moments, the plane was in the air and headed north.

Willard instinctively felt for his sidearm. One of the perks of being in the Bureau was being able to pack a loaded weapon onto an aircraft. If needed, he could have the revolver drawn and fired in one and a half seconds.

"I think we're being hi-jacked."

Baker looked at him in amazement. He glanced around the plane. He looked out the window and then back at Willard.

"You're crazy."

"Since when does it take four pilots to fly a plane this size?"

Baker pulled out his service revolver.

6

Lamech sat Indian-style on the police desk. His eyes were fixated on a missing child bulletin that was posted on a nearby wall. The information on the poster was minuscule, but to him, all of the tell-tale signs were there. Trouble was coming.

Rachel climbed out from the dark recesses under a desk three aisles away. She stepped from desktop to desktop. She stopped once and looked down at her feet.

"Sergeant Butler is so messy."

There was no reply, so she continued on her path until she came to a desk next to Lamech's. She sat down and studied him with her eyes. He still had not acknowledged her existence. A pen caught her attention. She picked it up to examine it more closely. She knew the pen would be missed. There would be accusations and hard feelings. The pen vanished.

"Will someone have to go?"

"Not someone, we." Lamech said without turning his attention away from the poster.

"Where are we going?"

"A place called Crescent City, California."

"California? I haven't been there since 1045. Do you suppose it's changed much?"

"I suppose so. It's populated now. People. Buildings. Roads. Just like here. Remember how it used to be here?"

"How soon do you want to get started?"

Lamech looked at the clock. It was three minutes to midnight. "Now."

Enos stepped out of the shadows in the corner by a supply closet. "Get started with what?"

"There's a problem in Crescent City, California." Rachel said.

"California? I haven't been there since 1429. Do you think it's changed much?"

"Duh." Rachel retorted.

"This is a good thing." Lamech said as he climbed off the desk and headed for the door. "I was beginning to hate Denver."

7:15 am. Peter sat at the large conference table. The top of the table was covered with sheets of paper. He had been up all night. Marty and Clark attempted to work through the night. Clark was the first to submit to exhaustion, and then Marty followed suit an hour later. Peter wasn't ready to give up. Turning the case over to someone else, in Peter's mind, was giving up.

There was a story here. A story with an ending. He just had to find it. Clark had made the suggestion to divide the case of the missing boy from the case of the missing police officer, but Peter rejected it. In his heart, he knew it was connected.

Captain Stockton stepped into the room. Peter could tell by the look on his face that he had more bad news. The Captain glanced at Clark, who had fallen asleep in one of the padded armchairs, and Marty, who had stretched out on the futon. He walked over to Peter and perched himself on the edge of the table. He sat there searching for the right words to say.

Since the Captain wasn't ready to speak, Peter decided he would initiate the conversation. "We're going to split the two cases up. The Bureau will investigate your missing officer. Clark and I will stay on and work the Miles case." Peter hoped it sounded like he wasn't giving them an option. He was prepared for an argument.

"That won't be necessary," The Captain said. "We've got a problem."

Peter thought of that as an understatement but felt it would be better not to say so.

"The plane carrying the boys from the Bureau has gone down. There's no sign of survivors."

Clark bolted upright. Marty sat up. Peter remained motionless, staring at the papers on the table.

"How soon before they send more men?" Peter asked.

"They won't for a while." Stockton said. "All of their available men will be committed to the plane crash." Stockton patted Peter on the shoulder, hopped off the table, and walked towards the door.

"Captain?" Peter turned his attention from the pile of papers. "Was any of the bodies found?"

"No. No survivors. No bodies. Just a badly wrecked plane."

Peter scribbled on a notepad, tore the sheet of paper free, and tossed it on the table with his other notes.

Clark came over and stood next to Peter's chair. "What do we do now?"

"We keep going."

Marty picked up the piece of paper that Peter had just added to the pile. She was surprised by the contents. "You think the plane crash is connected?"

"I do. Somehow, it's all connected."

"How?"

"I don't know yet." Peter replied. "But we'll find out. This much I'm sure."

"So what do we do now?" Clark was stretching the kinks out of his neck and back.

"I don't know. For the life of me, I honestly don't know. Let's go get a room at one of the hotels. Then let's try this on for size. I'll go back to the hospital to see if there is any change in Sarah Miles' condition. Why don't you and Marty go check on

Jones's wife? See if there's been any changes in his behavior, prior to his disappearance"

"Pete, buddy, Marty can do that by herself. Besides, I don't want to be the next person to disappear."

Marty tensed. Peter recognized Clark's humor, however there was an edge to Clark's voice. Peter had never known Clark to be so quick to judge.

"Just do it. Let's check back here in about two hours."

Marty started walking to the door. She stopped and turned to address Peter. "Sir, for what it's worth. I just really, really want to thank you for letting me..."

Peter raised an index finger in her general direction. He wagged his finger. "If you say that one more time, I swear to God, I'll have you back on the street."

"Okay, but... Okay."

Sarah Miles sat on the cot. Her emotional fits had ended, leaving her with dispair. Occasionally, she would get up and pace around the cold, generic room, but then she would return to the cot.

"Sarah? Do you feel like answering some questions?" Peter had to be cautious. The last thing he wanted to do was send her over the deep end.

Sarah looked up at him. Her eyes were blank and stained red from crying too many tears. When she spoke, it was in monotone.

"I will try."

"How do you feel?"

"Lost, alone. He's not coming back, is he?"

"I think it's a little early to give up hope. Sarah, what happened to the police officer?"

Sarah sat gazing at the cold, white walls. She said nothing.

"Sarah? Sarah. Do you remember?"

"Yes. I was looking for my son, Mikey. I could here his voice in my head. He was calling to me to come and find him.

Officer Jones was walking towards me. And then they came. They just stepped out of the dark."

"Who are they?"

"I don't know. Just people. They were dark. I couldn't see what they looked like."

"You said they were dark. Are you referring to their skin color? Or do you mean that it was too dark to see?"

"No. Neither. I could see them, but they looked like shadows walking around. I could see Officer Jones. I could see what he looked like, but..."

"Then what happened?"

"They grabbed him. They were standing all around him. You know, like a group hug, but then he wasn't there any more. And then the police car was coming. I could see the flashing lights. And those people just stepped back into the darkness."

Peter felt a chill crawl up the length of his spine. Fresh tears formed in Sarah's eyes. Her body trembled. She looked into Peter's eyes.

"Marty saved my life."

She laid down on the cot, curled up into a ball, and sobbed.

Peter stepped out of the hospital. The sun was still shining. Crescent City was notorious for it's fog and rain, but for a week now the skies have been uncommonly clear. The ocean breeze kept the town from warming up. It was too early in the season for swimming, picnics, and barbecues. But seeing the sun still helped to elevate the moods of most people, Peter included.

When he approached the car, he was surprised to see Clark and Marty standing there. He could tell that something was bothering them. Marty was leaning against her own car. Her hands were crammed into the pockets of her jacket. Since she had been cleared to work with the detectives, she was exempt from wearing her uniform. Peter silently admired her taste in wardrobe. In her business-like attire she still held on to her feminine charm. But now she stood there, avoiding making eye-contact with Clark or himself by staring at the ground.

Clark, on the other hand, was pacing slowly around the gold-colored cadillac. When he saw Peter approaching, he ceased his holding pattern and made a bee-line towards his partner. Marty followed, keeping some distance between Clark and herself, until they reached Peter.

Peter dug in his pocket for Clark's key to the hotel room. "We've got a view to the Safeway parking lot."

"You couldn't get the hotel by the harbor?"

"Are you paying?"

"No."

Peter shook his head. "It wasn't in the Department's price range. Besides, you're not planning on spending a lot of time there, are you?"

"Well, no. Of course not. Not now, anyway. I just thought that since this wasn't some crappy stakeout, they would splurge a little?"

Peter just laughed and shook his head. He looked at Marty and then at Clark. "So?"

"Well our trip was a complete washout." Clark said. "Did you find out anything?"

Peter quickly related Sarah Miles amazing story of shadow people who materialize and vanish in the dark.

"She's still sticking to her story, then?"

"Obviously, she's been traumatized, but she doesn't strike me as the type of person who would be easily fooled or confused." Peter looked to Marty for any input.

Marty broke away from Peter's eyes and returned her attention to a location in proximity to the asphalt. "She's a very level and rational person." Marty said in a voice only slightly louder than a whisper, and then she added, "at least for the most part, Sir."

Something was going on between Clark and Marty. Something must have happened while he was in the hospital. He was trying to figure the best approach to bring the subject up for discussion.

Clark interrupted his thought process. "On our way over here, Captain Stockton radioed. A night watchman never came home, this morning. His wife is concerned."

Peter ran his hands through his hair and sighed. "Let's go check it out."

"Do you think it's connected?" Marty searched his face for sincerity.

"Like I said earlier, it's all connected."

"I'll take my car. You guys can follow me. I know the way."

Mary sat on her bed and looked around the room. The bed was the only item that made the room resemble a bedroom. With the exception of a pathway to the door, the rest of the floorspace was committed to crates and boxes.

She decided to open the box marked 'clothes'. When she had packed it back in St. James, Missouri, she had left the clothes on the hangers to facilitate swifter packing and unpacking. Three more boxes and a half-hour later, The closet was filled. Her winter clothes were hung to the far left, then came her evening gowns. She placed her Sunday's bests on the rod, then her jeans and T-shirts. Her summer clothes came after that. Each hanger was placed a half of an inch apart.

She went to work on shoes. She went through pain-staking care to make sure each pair of shoes were matched, and the toes were pointed out. If the shoes had laces, they were tied. If the shoes had buckles, they were buckled. Slip-ons were for the lazy people and didn't exist in this household. There was barely enough room in the closet for her shoes. Mary paused for a moment to inspect her shoes. If she wanted to buy another pair she would have to decide which of the already existing pairs would have to be thrown out. That would come later.

She left the room and went to the top of the stairs.

"Daddy?" She called out.

"He's not here, honey. What do you need?"

"Mom, I'm finished with the closet. I want to set up my computer."

"Oh honey, couldn't you put your books away first?"

"It's going to take forever to set up the computer cabinet. I've got an idea for a story. I want to get it down before I forget."

"Couldn't you just write it down? You have all those notebooks."

"Yes, I suppose so. Can you help me assemble the bookcases?"

Her mom didn't answer. She waited. The fact that her mom hadn't answer didn't mean no.

"Mom?" Mary climbed halfway down the stairs. "Mom? What are you doing?" she reached the bottom of the staircase and turned into the living room. "Mom?"

"Oh, I'm sorry honey. What did you say?"

"Could you help me set up my bookcases?"

"Yeah honey, I was just going through some things."

"What are you looking for?"

"Huh?" Her mom had gone back to the box she was sorting through.

"Are you looking for something?"

"Yeah, uh-huh. Do you remember that time we went snorkeling in Hawaii? Hanauma Bay, right?

"Right. Yeah, that was a lot of fun. Why?"

"I thought we could go snorkeling here."

"Mom! The ocean is freezing this far north."

"I know, but summer is coming. And they have a river here that is suppose to be the second cleanest river in the United States."

"Really? Which one was number one?"

"You know what? They didn't say."

"It's probably the Meramec."

"Mary, I know you miss Missouri, but you'll see. You'll love it here. We're Californians now."

"Native Californians are people who are born in California. As far as California is concerned, we're still outsiders."

Mary sat down and started sorting through another box. "Where do you want the photo albums?"

"Third shelf. Chronological order."

"I know." She grabbed an armful of books sat them in their appropriate places. "Where's Dad?"

"You know your father. He's out doing a recon of the town."

Mary sat there for a moment. She wondered if it would be easier to do the work by herself, rather than wait for her mom to find a stopping point. She was about to act on her first impulse when there was a knock on the door.

"I'll get it." Mary said.

When she pulled the door open, she was greeted by a girl roughly the same age as she. The girl in the doorway looked as if she was a flashback from the sixties. She wore beads in her hair, which was loosely covered by a funky denim hat. She wore a tie-dyed T-shirt, faded jeans, and sandals.

Okay, Mary thought to herself, so retro is in.

"Dude, I've been waiting for you to come out, so we could bump into each other accidentally. But you've been in here for ever."

"I'm sorry. I've been unpacking."

"That's okay. My name is Kayla."

"Hi, my name is Mary. Won't you come in? You wouldn't happen to be handy with tools, would you?"

"Dude, no way. Why?"

"I'm trying to put my bookshelves together. Do you think you could hold them together? I'll operate the screwdriver."

"I guess we could try."

Mary led Kayla to her room. After about an hour, Kayla gave up. She sat down on the bed and glanced around at the boards, brackets, and assortments of pins and screws that would eventually resemble a bookshelf.

"Hey, is your phone hooked up, yet?"

"Not until tomorrow, why?"

"I'll be right back. I know just the person for the job."

When Kayla returned, she brought three of her friends with her. "Hey Dude, this is Roger, T-Jack, and Rosie. Guys, meet Mary."

Mary was a little uncertain about having so many strangers in her house at one time, let alone in her room. But she wanted to have her bedroom sat up before she went to bed. She knew her dad — It would be hours before he returned from his recon. If he had any complaints, she would tell him that she was delegating her authority. He would understand that.

T-Jack and roger sat up the computer cabinet in a little under two hours. When it was completed, Mary and T-Jack sat up the computer, with all of its auxiliaries and accessories. Roger moved on to setting up the entertainment stand and three sets of bookshelves. After putting the computer cabinet together, the rest was a breeze. Kayla assisted Roger, if only minimally. Rosie busied herself by gathering up the boxing materials and straps.

"So, where are you from, Mary?" T-Jack's voice came from behind the cabinet.

"A little bit of everywhere. Daddy was an Army colonel. Everywhere he went, we followed. I was born in Germany. When I was three, he was stationed at Fort Sam Houston, Texas. Let's see, Korea, Hawaii, and Fort Leonard Wood, Missouri. Everybody calls it Fort Lost-in-the-Woods, Misery. He's retired now."

"So what brings you to Crescent City?" Roger didn't want to be left out of the conversation.

"My mom and dad met in Fort Carson, Washington. She was in the nursing corp. He was wounded in Beirut. The Army sent daddy to Madigan Hospital to recuperate. It was love at first sight. They were married, and they drove down to San Francisco for their honeymoon. When they drove through

Crescent City, they vowed that this is where they would live when they retired."

"Aww. That is so sweet." Rosie swooned.

By the time Mary and T-Jack had the computer sat up, Roger had finished putting together the last bookcase. T-Jack went to work setting up the stereo system and all of its accessories. The rest of the small group loaded books on the shelves.

"I don't want to sound anal-retentive, but I like to put the books in sections of authors, and then in alphabetical order, according to the titles."

"Dude, I've seen your closet. You are very anal." Kayla retorted.

"Hella-retentive." Roger added, nodding his head.

"Hey, guys. Organization is the key to success." Mary said in her own defense.

"Really?" Kayla piped back.

"Yes, really."

"Actually, Einstein used to say that a messy desk was a sign of an intelligent mind." T-Jack said without looking up from his work.

"True. But I would be willing to bet you that his desk only appeared messy to other people. To him, it was all organized in his mind."

"Touche." T-Jack said.

"So tell me about Crescent City."

Roger was all too happy to get his two-cents worth in to the conversation. "What's to know? A majority of the population is school-aged kids and old folks. There's nothing to do around here, so most people move away when they graduate. But then they always come back to raise their own kids."

"Most of the kids around here get hooked on pot or 'shrooms." Kayla added. "Every now and then, we get a couple of cases of beer and hang out at the jetty, at night."

"What's the jetty?" Mary was thinking of discos and nightclubs.

"It's the breakwater down by the lighthouse. They built it to keep the larger waves from damaging the boats in the harbor. It's made of these large cement blocks called tetrapods. You'll see." Kayla said.

"It's so much fun." Rosie said. "We drink, play hide and seek, or tetrapod tag."

"What about the police?'

"It's no big deal." Roger said. "Most of the cops are cool. Some of them are real dicks, though."

"Officer Martinez." Kayla sighed.

"Marty's the biggest dick of them all." Rosie added.

"He is?"

"Not he. Marty's a she." T-Jack was trying to untangle a coil of speaker wires.

"Oh."

7

"We're going to have problems with her."

"What do you mean?" Peter was surprised at how easily it was to get his partner to open up.

"She forgets that we are the trained detectives. The whole time we were interrogating her partner's wife, Amy Jones, she kept trying to dominate the conversation. I still haven't ruled her out as a suspect. It's a mistake to have her involved in the investigation."

"For the record, I don't consider her a suspect. She probably figured she knows Mrs. Jones better than we. Try to show some compassion. She did just lose a partner."

"That's another thing. I don't see any remorse. It's as if she's just a little bit too mechanical about it. If it weren't for this fantastic story by an eyewitness, who just so happens to be certifiably touched in the head, There's no way you could convince me that Marty didn't do it."

"Okay, I'll talk to her about letting go of the reins a bit. On the other hand, if she were a suspect, and she's not, but if she were, what better place to have her than close at hand."

"You're right." Clark said reluctantly.

"Let's have her do the questioning on this one. Let's see what happens."

"You're the boss."

Marty's car pulled up to the curb in front of a house on Gainard avenue. Peter pulled the Cadillac in behind Marty's car. When Peter climbed out, Marty was already standing by.

"How do you want to handle this one?"

"Marty, this is your lucky day. Clark and I are going to be observers only."

"Really? Really? Sir, I promise I won't let you down."

"Okay, one small point, but an important one." Peter looked at Marty first, then Clark, and then back at Marty. "Please don't call me 'Sir' or 'Boss' anymore. It's so annoying."

"I never called you 'Boss'." Marty said, defensively.

"No, that was me." Clark said.

Marty led the way up the driveway. She took the three steps of the porch, one step at a time. Her body was fully erect and poised as if she was a beauty pageant contestant taking her final stroll across the stage.

She pressed the doorbell button. After a moment, she glanced back as if to ensure that her newly acquired partners hadn't deserted her in a cruel ruse of ding-dong ditch. Once she had assured herself that she was not alone, she pressed the button again.

A lady, still dressed in a nightgown and housecoat, came and answered the door. She was a mousy little character, about twenty-three. Her face was creased with worry. After showing Marty and the detectives in and offering them a seat, she lit a fresh cigarette with the butt of the last cigarette that she had just smoked to the quick.

"You'll have to excuse me. I don't usually smoke this much."

"That's fine." Marty gave a sideways glance towards Clark. Satisfied that he wasn't going to interfere, she continued. "Mrs. Alden, we need to ask you some questions. Are you feeling up to it?"

"Yeah, sure. If it will help find my husband. You haven't heard anything?"

Marty shook her head. "No, Ma'am."

"Be honest now. Would you tell me if you had?"

"If we had, we wouldn't be sitting here now."

"Okay."

"Has there been any changes in your husband's behavior in the last couple of weeks?"

"No."

"Could you give us an example of an average day?"

"He goes to work at 10:30 in the evening. He's usually home by 7:30 in the morning. We lay down together for about three to four hours. I get up, but he usually sleeps until one or two in the afternoon. He watches TV for awhile. Then he takes a nap from 7:00 to 9:00. Then he's off to work again."

"He never goes out?"

"Well, yeah. Sometimes, he runs to the store for me, other errands, you know, stuff like that. But he's mostly a homebody. That's why I knew something was wrong."

"Excuse me for asking, but how is your sex life?"

"Good. Great. Well, you know, he never complains." Mrs. Alden blushed moderately.

Marty looked towards Peter. She shrugged slightly. She had no idea where to go from there.

Peter spoke. "Ma'am, I have one last question. Has he taken any large amounts of money out of your checking or savings accounts? Are you missing anything of value?"

Mrs. Alden looked up in surprise. "As a matter of fact, there is three hundred dollars missing. One of my girlfriends told me that I should check our accounts. He pulls out a twenty now and then, but he always tells me about it."

"I'm sorry, one more question. Who usually does the finances?"

"I do, for the most part."

"And the three hundred dollars is the only thing missing?"

"Yes. Do you think he used the money to leave?"

"If he did, he wouldn't get far. But you will let us know if you notice anything else missing, won't you?"

"Yes, of course. So you think he ran away?"

"Ma'am, it's to early to speculate anything."

Peter made eye contact with Clark, and then Marty. Neither seemed to have any more questions. Peter made a quick survey of the living room. "Very well then. Ma'am, we thank you for your time. We'll let you know if we find anything."

"Thank you." She said. She stood up to see them to the door. "He's all right, right? I mean, he's not in trouble or anything? He hasn't broken any law, and he hasn't ran off with some girl. I know this."

Marty spoke this time. "It's too early to tell. The best thing for you to do now is not give up hope." As soon as she said it, she realized that it probably wasn't the most appropriate words to say. She felt loss.

"Okay, thank you." Mrs. Alden said, choking back a sob. She lit another cigarette, then walked with them to the door. Once they reached the door, she spoke through a cloud of smoke. "You'll let me know as soon as you find him?"

"I promise." Peter said.

When they had made their way to their cars, Peter handed his keys over to Clark. "I'm going to ride with Marty.

Clark nodded in affirmative.

As Marty steered the car towards the Police Station, Peter talked to her. "So, how is everything with you?"

"Okay." She said, keeping her eyes on the road. "How do you think the investigation is going?"

"It's like you said. It's too early to tell. What I'm curious about is how you and Clark are getting along."

"Oh please. I know you told me not to mention it again, but I really am thankful that you let me be on your team. I know you're going out on a limb by doing so. I don't want to do anything to jeopardize this opportunity."

"I'm not going so far out on any limb. You were highly recommended by your Captain. If I thought there was a problem, you wouldn't be here now. I don't take risks. So, how are things between you and Clark?"

"Sir, you don't take risks. I don't gossip, and I don't talk about my working companions behind their backs."

"Good answer. But if there is a problem with my team, we resolve them. Obviously, there's tension. I want to clear it up."

"Sir, I just want to say that I'm professional enough to work with people that I don't get along with. I really appreciate this opportunity. I promise, I'll try not to upset the balance in your team."

"So answer the question."

"Sir, I'm in a lose-lose situation here. If I tell you what's going on, then I'm branded as a trouble-maker, or worse, insubordinate. If I could prove that I'm being professional here, then I'll be causing tension between you and your partner. And your investigation will suffer for it."

"Do me a favor. Try this on for size. My name is Peter. Call me Peter."

"Peter."

"Thank you. Now answer the question."

"I think Clark is very professional at what he does. You're both good at what you do. It's an honor for me to see such proficiency and dedication at work."

"Fine. But you're not telling me what I want to hear."

Marty sank in the driver's seat. She realized she could no longer avoid the question. One way or the other she was going to be off the team and back on the street. "What's to say? I think he's rude, obnoxious, and arrogant. I heard what he said about me doing my partner in. I would never do that. He jumped all over me, when I was asking Amy questions about her husband. I wasn't trying to step on anybody's toes. I just thought that since I knew Amy personally..." She was so mad that she felt tears welling up. She had said too much.

Peter hadn't intended on upsetting her. He thought it better to not make an issue of her emotional stress. However, he was visibly relieved that she had opened up to him.

"Now, you see. That's the odd part. I've known Clark most of my life. I've never seen him like this." Peter looked over at

Marty. Suddenly, it was as if he was noticing her for the first time.

"Oh my God! Why didn't I see it before?"

"What?"

"He's infatuated with you."

"What? No way!"

"I know him. It's the only logical answer. I'll bet my bottom dollar on it."

"Great! What will his wife say when she finds out?"

"It's kind of hard to say. She died of leukemia, ten years ago."

"I am so sorry. I didn't know." Marty continued to keep her eyes glued to the road.

"He hasn't dated anybody since. I don't thinks he's even noticed another woman. Man, I can't believe I didn't catch that."

"So, Okay, um. What's your story?"

"What do you mean?"

"Oh, don't act so surprised. You have divorced written all over you."

"Me? I'm nothing. When I was still a rookie, I started taking classes so I could move up to detective. I was going to school full-time and working full-time. My wife met a guy on the Internet. And that was the end of that."

"So your career came before your family?"

"I guess so. In my heart, I thought I was making a better life for us. Have you ever heard about the man who crossed the hottest desert, swam the deepest ocean, and climbed the highest mountain just to prove to his wife how much he loved her?"

"No."

"She divorced him anyway. The bum was never home.

"Oh, no. How sad."

"The irony of it all, is that I would've been just as happy being a street cop. I've always been so jealous of Clark. He had such a happy marriage. Marriages are suppose to end with 'until death do you part'. Divorce is a way of saying you failed."

Marty tensed. "This ex-Mrs. Swann, she's still alive, right? You're not needing to make a confession now, are you?"

Peter chuckled. "No. She's alive. I'm over her."

"I'm kind of like that. I want to settle down, but I want to be more secure in my career first. I mean, have I accomplished everything I'm capable of? If I get involved with some guy, it will only get in the way of my goals."

"Unless your goals are to find the right person to spend the rest of your life with."

Marty didn't respond. She pulled the car up to the little cobblestone building that housed the Crescent City Police Department.

After they had vacated their cars, they adjourned to the conference room. Peter grabbed his notepad and pen. he began jotting down key points from the last three interviews. When he had finished writing, he sat the pen down on the table. Marty and Clark stood on the other side of the immense table. The paper work from earlier was left undisturbed. Captain Stockton made it clear to other officers that until the investigation was finished, the conference room was off limits to everyone but these three.

"What if..." Peter finally spoke.

"What if?" Clark prodded.

"What if..." Peter paused again. "Okay, I need you both to promise to hear me out, and not have me locked up."

"Partner, what have you got cooking in that noggin?"

"Let's say that the Miles woman isn't crazy. What if we're dealing with some kind of supernatural forces, here."

"Marty, call the boys in the white coats."

"Sir, Peter, Sir. I have to agree with Clark with this one." Marty was reluctant to take Clark's side, but under the circumstances, she felt it a necessity.

"Pete, buddy. Are you looking for some time off?"

"No, I don't think so."

"You haven't had any sleep since we got here. I think you should get some rest."

"Wait a minute. Sirs uh, Guys, now I don't believe in the supernatural, but that aside, what if we were dealing with a person, or persons, that did? What if we were dealing with a group of people who wanted the town to think that the supernatural was involved?" Marty was relieved to be somewhat back on Peter's side and not Clark's.

"Exactly. Just what are we dealing with? A little boy, a police officer, a security guard, four FBI agents, two pilots and a stewardess." Peter shook his head. He drummed his fingers on the table, picked up his pen and twirled the end of it between his lips, sat the pen down, and began drumming his fingers again.

"Maybe it's a league of Satan worshippers, Sir."

"Is that a possibility?" Clark looked incredulously at Marty. "What about this? What if it is a team of terrorists?"

"That's a possibility too, Sir, but it's not a probability in a small town like Crescent City."

"When I was young..." Peter was still staring at the pile of papers in front of him. "I was terrified of the dark. My dad used to tell me there's nothing in the dark that isn't in the light."

"Your dad must have never been camping." Clark said. "Bears come out at night. Wolves come out at night. Even owls and field mice come out at night."

"Clark's right, Sir um, Peter. A great deal of offenders use the darkness of night to conceal their crimes."

"I know that, now. But what if there is something else out there. Something that is in the dark that isn't in the light."

"Pete, buddy. You're starting to sound like the Miles woman."

"So what if I am? How many more lives are going to be affected before this is through? Whether or not this is natural or supernatural, how many lives can we save and protect?"

"What are you suggesting?"

"We need a county-wide curfew, from sundown to dawn. We shut down any establishment that is open all night. Nothing moves except law enforcement and security."

"You forget. Law enforcement and security are already a part of the casualties." Clark could tell that Peter was scared. It was unsettling to see him this way.

"Yes. But according to the reports, the night watchman clocked out for lunch and left the building. And Jones was looking for a civilian. Whether this is real or not, we need that curfew."

"Pete, buddy. You've been up a long time. I've actually gotten some sleep. As your friend, I'm urging you to go back to the hotel room and get some rest. Just don't run anybody over on your way back to the hotel."

"Your not going to leave it alone, are you." Peter was too tired to banter.

"Peter, Sir, I'm in the same condition as Clark. I've had some sleep. You haven't had any."

"Are you guys up to this?" Peter waited for them to nod. "Okay then. Get the curfew in effect. Do me a favor. Check out any Satanic activities. Also, find out any local legends. This area is filled with Indian heritage. Let's meet back here by 22:30. Make sure you get some rest."

"Sir, there's something else. When we were looking for Sarah Miles, we were parked out at the fisherman's dock. Jones said he heard something and took us straight to her. From where we were, it was impossible for him to have heard her."

Peter stood up, walked around the table, and laid his hands on her shoulder. He waited to speak until she looked up into his eyes. "Don't beat yourself up over this." With that said, he walked out of the room.

"He's like that, you know." Clark said, after Peter had left. "Even when we're on stakeouts, he leaves the TV on. Kind of like having a night light."

Las Vegas was lit up as usual. Lamech had read in someone's newspaper once that one could see the lights of Vegas in the night sky, as far away as Phoenix, Arizona. He believed that it must be true. But even though Vegas was brighter than the average city, Lamech felt it would be better to stick to the larger cities for the time being.

The commotion caused in Crescent City could alert Mortals to their existence. He knew that a band of rebels were forming. For the survival of the majority, this rebel faction would have to be squashed.

Though they were capable of leaping great distances in the dark, they still had limitations. The sun would be rising in a couple of hours. They would have to find a dark recess soon. It would not be good to be caught in the desert at dawn.

Rachel appeared just left of him. "It will be morning soon. We need to assimilate."

"We will find it there." He said, pointing across the desert towards the lights.

Willie Bronson was not ready to go home. He had money in his pocket, and he was horny. He loved his wife, but she just didn't understand him. He wasn't cheating on her. He was only performing a function check on his equipment.

He had been driving the strip for a couple of hours. None of the girls appealed to him. "Who am I kidding? I'm just scared." He said out loud. Coming to this realization only made him more determined. He drove two more blocks and pulled over.

A young lady, scantily dressed in a way that Willie thought was tacky, knocked on his window. When she opened the door and climbed in, She asked "Are you looking for someone?"

"You'll do." He said. Then he drove to a darkened alley away from the strip. It would be easier to discuss business there. They climbed into the back of his Pontiac '86 Sunbird.

"Whatcha got in mind, Babe?"

"What's on the menu?"

"Menu? Thaz cute. Well anyways, umm. A handjob is fifteen. Blowjobs are twenty. Around the world is an extra ten. You can go down on me for twenty, and around the world is another ten. Or we could go all the way for fifty. I don't do golden showers, and absolutely no rear entries."

Willie reached for his wallet. Suddenly the young lady hisscd.

"Stop! It's the Cops."

Both of the back doors flew open simultaneously. Willie hid his face with his arms, in a feeble attempt to prolong being identified. His wife was going to be crushed when she found out. He would never be able to look her in the eyes again.

The lady had a different thought. Having had experiences at being arrested, she realized that something was not right. For example, if these were Las Vegas' finest, why couldn't she make out any features. They didn't say "You're under arrest." or "You have the rights to remain silent." And another thing, instead of pulling her and her client out of the car, these guys were climbing in. It's as if they meant to sit on the occupants' laps.

And then the lady and her customer became cold. Very, very cold.

When Las Vegas' Finest found the car, later that morning, the keys were still in the ignition, the owner's wallet was on the back seat with a large sum of money still inside, and so was a purse that belonged to a well-known streetwalker. The owners of the wallet and purse was no where to be found.

No one thought to explore a drainpipe that was situated a few feet further in the alley.

Darla Lovesyou sat on the floor with her legs crossed. On the coffee table, in front of her, was a missing child bulletin and a newspaper clipping. The article from the Crescent City's Triplicate was sketchy, at best. But, for what the article didn't say, she already knew. She had seen everything in a vision.

Her life was in danger. The Umai could not allow her to exist. As the grand-daughter to the last great medicine woman of the Yurok nation, it was her position to make a stand against the Umai. She was not ready.

Other people would be coming soon. The Authorities would be asking her questions. She wasn't sure if she was prepared to answer them. And if she did answer the Authorities' questions, How much should she reveal? How much did they need to know? How much were they willing to believe? And more importantly, how much could she handle on her own, without their help or interference?

She made up her mind. When the sun came up, She would have to seek advice from the Council. She hoped that the Authorities didn't come for her before that. And she prayed that the Umai didn't come at all.

8

School was out, but Mary felt no need to hurry home. She ambled along the sidewalk, taking in the scenery. St. James, Missouri was a cute little town, and there was plenty to do, if one were to apply themselves. But St. James didn't have anything on Crescent City. Crescent City had an ocean at the front door and large, beautiful redwoods at the back door. The town folk were more friendly. The weather didn't go through the extremes of too hot to too cold. It wasn't difficult to see why her parents wanted to settle down here. She even vowed to learn to appreciate seafood, but that might be pushing it.

She had walked a block from the school, when the others finally caught up with her.

"Dude, did you here the announcement on the intercom?" Kayla was being her bubbly self.

"No. What was it?"

"Del Norte County is going on a curfew, starting at sundown, tonight."

"Isn't that just like Crescent City? One little boy comes up missing, and the whole town shuts down." Roger said.

"So what does that mean?" Mary was worried that they had plans that would include her. She was right.

"Dude, that means we'll have the whole town to ourselves." Kayla seemed just a little too excited.

"Hey, that's right." T-Jack said. The excitement appeared to be spreading. "This would be the perfect night to hang out at the Jetty."

"Oh! Oh, no! My dad would kill me if I got in trouble with the law." Mary protested.

Roger laughed. "God, the cops in this town are such a joke."

"They ain't gonna do nothing." T-Jack joined in.

"Hey dude, besides, you only live once." Everyone laughed. Everyone except Mary.

"Dude." T-Jack said to Roger. "Do you still have those cases of beers stashed?"

"Even if I didn't, I could always get some more. We gonna toke it tonight?"

"Yeah, that would be so cool." Kayla retained her high level of elation. "But try to get some better stuff. That last batch gave me a headache."

"I better not, guys. I've got a project I'm working on." Mary lied, though it wasn't a big lie. Her project was to live to see twenty.

"Aw, come on. Don't be lame." Kayla urged.

"Man, hella-lame, if you ask me." Rosie finally spoke, but then she fell silent again.

Roger threw his arm around Mary's shoulders, and in staged whisper, he said, "I'll make it worth your while."

Roger was cute. His brassy attitude repulsed her, but she felt a surge of emotions in the pit of her stomach. Against her better judgment, she nodded in agreement.

"We're headed down to the Cutting Board. You want to come along?" Kayla was relieved that Mary had given in.

"No, if I'm going to violate my parents' trust, I better go home and take care of some business, first."

"Right on. God, what a weird concept. We'll meet you at the park by ten, okay?"

"Okay, but if I'm not there, go on without me."

"Whatever." Kayla said, putting emphasis on each syllable.

"You'll be there." Roger said, as he released his hold on her.

Rosie put her hand on Mary's arm. "He likes you. You are all he keeps talking about."

"Really?"

"Uh huh."

They walked on without her. A few minutes later, she was alone again. She wasn't pleased with herself, but she couldn't have Roger thinking she was lame. She picked up her pace. If she was going to see him tonight, she had a lot to do.

She thought there might be a story here, but she couldn't think of one at the moment.

"Honey, are you all right?"

"Yes, Mom. Why do you ask?"

"Well, it's just that you've been so busy since you've been home. Do you have plans for later? You haven't said anything."

"No, we can't. They've got a county-wide curfew that's taking effect tonight."

"Really?" I hadn't heard."

"I just felt like helping out."

"Okay, where's my real daughter? What have you done with her?"

"Oh, stop it. I help out."

"Yes you do. You're a sweetheart." Her mother turned to walk back into the kitchen. "Are you sure you're okay?"

"I'm fine. Do you need any help in the kitchen?"

"I could use some company."

A few minutes later, Mary was slicing carrots. They had to be cut at just the right angle to facilitate cooking in the stir-fry. She enjoyed medial chores like this. Her mind could wander away to the stories that she was writing. But this time, instead of stories, she thought of Roger. He was at least a foot taller than she, and it was clear that he worked out. She thought of how good it felt to be in his arms. She wondered if it had meant anything to him.

He would have to change. She had no intentions of hanging out with a booze hound. And Marijuana always leads to harder drugs. She had read that in a pamphlet, somewhere.

"Is it a boy?"

"What?"

"Just now. You had a quirky smile on your face."

"I did?"

"Yes. Do you want to talk about it?"

"Well... There is someone who might be interested in me. But it's way too early to tell."

"Is it Roger or T-Jack?"

"How do you know it's either?"

"Those are the only two that's been over here, so unless there's someone at school..." Her mother baited.

"No. It's Roger." Mary said reassuring her.

"He's handsome enough, and he seems nice. Just don't let your father find out. You know how he is about his little princess growing up too fast."

"Fathers! Who ever invented them?" Mary teased.

"Actually, they were invented before... never mind. You will be careful, won't you?"

"Mom, I'm not going to do anything stupid."

"God, I wish I could be you again."

"Don't be silly. Who would be you?"

"No one. Your father would have to do without."

Mary kissed her mother on the cheek. "I'll be up in my room if you need me."

"Okay, honey. We'll call you when dinner is ready."

Mary spent the rest of the evening tidying up her room. She worked on her stories. At a quarter to eight, she jumped into the shower. She changed her clothes completely, three times. She finally settled on jeans and her yellow top.

Dinner was delicious. Stir-fry was a favorite, complete with chopsticks, rice, and green tea. Mom and Dad drank sake. Mary had some once, but someone told her that since rice doesn't have juice, sake is made by old women chewing on rice and spitting in bottles. So sake is technically fermented saliva. She has never had a chance to check reality on that story, but she's never been able to drink the stuff since then. either.

Dad kept the conversation light. Above the table, Mary was as content as a nursing kitten. Below the table, where her father couldn't see, her feet were wagging, rapidly.

When she had eaten all that she could, she used her napkin to clear away any food particles that may have escape her mouth. She sat the napkin down and folded her hands in her lap.

The dinner conversation had dried up. An occasional ting of drinking glasses lent a musical quality to the silence. The clock in the hallway, usually mute, was pounding out the seconds.

"I think I'm going to step outside for a little while." Mary could bear the noise no longer.

"Mary, stay close. There's a curfew on the whole town."

"Really, Dad? I hadn't heard."

Mary exchanged glances with her mother. She excused herself from the table, grabbed her jacket out of the hallway closet, and stepped out into the night.

The town had taken on an eerie calm. There was no traffic. No city noise. Lights were on in each of the houses, but there was no other evidence of the occupants. "They did it! They shut down the whole town!"

Darla Lovesyou sat in her den. She was troubled that the Authorities arrived before she had a chance to talk to the Council. The fact that it was only one person, when she was expecting at least three, confused her. Then it occurred to her. This isn't over.

She told the plainclothes policewoman everything she knew. It seemed like the right thing to do, at the time. If they needed more, they would be in touch. Something told her that they would need more. So she spent the rest of the evening studying her limited collection of books on Native American folklore.

This wasn't over. Not by a long shot.

9

7:45 PM. HBO was playing a movie he had seen a hundred times. Those kind of movies were the best kind of movies to sleep through. He took comfort in knowing the story line, like a favorite bedtime story.

He kept one of the hotel's pillows folded and pressed under his head. He wrapped his arms around the other pillow and held it close to his chest. Many nights were dreamless. Many nights, the stories and actions played out on the television fused their way into his dreams. All too often, he dreamt of his ex-wife, of better times, or reunions that were never going to happen.

This evening was different. He was in a forest. There were voices all around him, sinister voices that foretold great harm. Everywhere he looked, glowing yellow eyes pierced the darkness. Human-shaped shadows, darker than the night, were reaching for him. They were calling him by name.

He sat up, startled from his sleep. He grabbed the sheet, the blankets, the pillows. And then he placed a hand on his chest. His heart was racing, and his breathing was labored. He was bathed in cold perspiration.

Just as he began to regain control of his senses, the dream became real. Someone was sitting at the foot of his bed. He dug his heels into the mattress and shoved until his back was pressed against the cold wall.

"Nightmare?" Clark finally spoke.

"Oh God, It's you."

"No, it's just me. Have a bad dream?"

"It was so real."

"You want to talk about it?"

"No, absolutely not. I was walking through a forest. Everything was dark. All of a sudden, I was surrounded. They were trying to get me."

"Well, okay then. If you're sure you don't want to talk about it."

"You're such an asshole. So what's going on."

"I've sent Marty on a wild goose chase."

"What kind of wild goose chase?"

"Oh, you know. Pretty much everything you asked us to do."

"Is the curfew being established?"

"Even as we speak. You know, Pete. We've been up against some tough cases before. I've never seen you like this."

"What do you mean?" Peter got out of bed and made his way to the sink. He poured himself a glass of water. When he drained it, he poured himself another.

"You are spooked."

Peter returned and sat on the bed. HBO was starting another movie. This one was about a young boy who conjures up his favorite Martial Arts hero to help him overcome his own shortcomings.

"It's the Miles woman. She wasn't out of it, this time. She spoke evenly. She was cognitive and coherent."

"It's the drugs. We've dealt with this before."

"I know that. But this isn't someone who's popping pills, or someone who is strung out on heroine. This isn't someone who got plastered drunk, climbed up on a sink, and cut themselves trying to shave their rump in the mirror."

"Clark chuckled. "That was an interesting case, wasn't it?"

"Something drove her over the deep side."

"You don't think losing a child could do that?"

"Well, yes I do. That, and whatever happened to Jones."

Clark stood up, walked over to his own bed, and flopped down. "I'm going to get some sleep. Marty's going to meet us here. Are you going to be able to go back to sleep?"

"I'll try."

The kid on TV was being beaten up by three other kids, while the girl of his dreams stood helplessly watching.

"Hey Clark, before you doze off, there's something I've been meaning to talk to you about."

"What's that?"

"What do you think about Marty?"

"She's bright, smart, very determined. She's kind of cute and charming. Very professional. Why do you ask?"

"You've been riding her a little rough."

"I don't know why I do it." Clark said sheepishly. "It's just that every time I'm near her, things go hay-wired inside me. I haven't felt this way since..."

"Since Penelope passed away?"

"Yeah."

"I know." Peter said.

"I never have problems concentrating. You know me. But now, all I can do is think of her."

"Someone once said 'My mind never wanders. I just send it on errands'."

"Yeah." Clark chuckled. "That sounds like me all right. Do you know who said it?"

"Yes, as a matter of fact, I do. It was some guy by the name of Tony Perkins."

"The Actor?"

"Naw, the other guy. The writer."

"Oh."

They laid there for a moment. Both were staring at the ceiling, watching the lights from the television play out a Technicolor aurora borealis. They were lost in their own thoughts for a moment.

"So you have feelings for her?"

"Yeah, I guess I do."

The kid in the movie was explaining to his imaginary hero that the instructions were impossible to follow.

"What gave me away?" Clark continued.

"The fact that you were trying not to give anything away."

"What do I do now?"

"Now, you should sleep. But later, maybe you could see if she wants to go to lunch. Ask her if she knows a good place."

"Yeah, that might work." Clark waited a moment. "Hey Pete?"

"I'm not listening to you."

"All right."

If she were to close her eyes and fall to sleep, at that moment, she would only get four hours of sleep. Who could sleep? Marty wondered if she should run the information over to the hotel room at that moment, or could it wait for later?

She decided to wait. If they were asleep, what she had to tell them would only keep them from going back to sleep. They needed their rest.

She thought about working out, but that idea was vetoed. She was too exhausted to benefit from exercising. Aerobics would keep her awake.

The warm spray from the shower head felt good. It helped her to relax, a little. She had to double-check the locks on all the doors and windows. And she had made sure that all the lights in the house were on, before she could climb into the tub. Using great care, she was able to direct the stream of the hand-held nozzle away from spraying on the bathroom floor. She was too concerned, not afraid, to close the shower curtain.

Normally, she would have stayed in longer. It's better to not tempt fate. So she turned off the water, stepped out onto the mat, and wrapped herself into a bath blanket.

In her bedroom, she exchanged the over-sized towel for an over-sized T-shirt. She contemplated which panties to wear. The hem of the T-shirt fell down almost to her knees, and panties were confining.

She made another sweep of the little one-bedroom home. This time, she rechecked the locks on the doors and windows, and turned out the lights as she went. Once she was back in the sanctuary of her room, she glanced at the clock. It was seven. On the other side of the heavy blanket that served as a curtain, the spring sun still hadn't set.

She climbed on the bed, placed a pillow between her back and the wall, pulled the blankets up around her hips, and placed the phone on her lap. She wasn't sure who she should call, but it felt important to make contact with someone.

Since her father was diagnosed with Parkinson's disease, coupled with Rheumatoid Arthritis, her parents moved away to the warmer climate of Phoenix. Captain Stockton and his wife all but adopted her. She couldn't call them. She thought about calling the two detectives. Once again, she turned down that idea, in case they were able to sleep. She dialed the number to the house in Arizona and held her breath.

"Hi Mom. It's me."

"I was just calling to see how you and Dad are doing."

"Well, yes. But Mom, clinical trials are important. And since they're paying for the medications..."

"How did you hear about the Miles boy? Yes, but since I'm working on the case, you know I can't talk about..."

"Yes, he's still missing. Yes, she's still in the hospital."

"I can't talk about that."

"I just called to see how you and Dad were doing."

"Yes I do."

"I do too."

"Nothing's wrong."

"I do too."

"Well, can you blame me? Look at how this conversation is going."

"As a matter of fact, I have met a guy."

"No. I'm not pregnant."

"Mom!"

"I just met him."

"I'm hanging up now."

"Tell Dad I love him."

"Mom, if you don't hear from me for a while... I love you, too."

"Okay, bye."

She replaced the phone on the nightstand and slid down under the covers. As she closed her eyes, she thought about him, his face, his eyes, his hands. She prayed that nothing bad would happen while she slept, so she could see him one more time.

When the alarm went off at ten, she bolted up in bed. He was still on her mind. she wasn't even certain she had fallen to sleep. This was stupid. This was so not like her. She didn't have any room in her life for a man. She had to get back on track.

She was annoying him again. Why couldn't she see how close he was to the breaking point? Gerard Pinchuck wasn't sure how much more he was going to be able to take.

Admittedly, it wasn't necessarily her fault. She was just there. She was always just there. A man could suffocate if he didn't have his space.

On the other hand, Petra was not a woman to leave home. The stupid broad was always changing things, twiddling with things, rearranging things. It infuriated him the way she couldn't leave well enough alone.

And she was stupid. Like that time, when he came home, and she was just sitting there watching TV. And he calmly asked her about dinner. She actually told him she was afraid of making the wrong meal. Well, nobody was going to live under the roof that he worked so hard to pay for and mouth off to him. That mouth of hers was always getting her in trouble, so the way he saw it, he was doing her a favor by slapping that mouth of hers. She overreacted by falling to the ground. When he tried to pull her up by her arm, he felt something give. Her arm had become dislocated at the shoulder... Okay, that was his fault.

But the stupid twit should have never fell down. That was three years ago.

Three years later, she was still annoying him.

"Gerry, are we going home now?"

"Is that what you want? You want to go home now?"

"I don't care. Whatever you want." Petra realized too late that she should have kept quiet and been content to follow him.

"Why don't you make up your mind." Gerard was getting irate. "I go through all the trouble of taking you to a nice restaurant and a movie. What do you do? You complain the whole night." His voice pitched. "And you threw up in the movies."

"You know I get sick in gory movies."

"You make me sick. Why don't you go home?"

"But, Gerry..."

"Go! Get out of here!" Gerard gave his wife a shove in the direction of their apartment. He stomped off towards Baxter's Grill and Bar. The Tinsel Town Cinema was only four blocks away from where they lived. The dumb woman could easily make it home. It was only dark for two or three blocks. Let's face it, twenty-seven was too old for a chick to be afraid of the dark. This would be good. This would get the ninny to grow up.

Medford was a beautiful city. The air was clean. The ground was free of litter. The whole city had a scrubbed, almost sterile appearance, compared to other cities that Lamech had visited.

Crescent City was a hop, skip, and jump away, literally. Lamech had made the decision to stay in Medford, overday. Time was short, but timing was essential. They would have to be in top form, the moment they stepped into Crescent City.

They stayed in the shadows of trees that decorated the grounds of a nursing home. There were people inside that would be easy pickings. But each and everyone would be missed. Any one of the residents would draw attention if they were to come up missing, too much attention. With what was going on in Crescent City, any attention could be lethal to his kind.

From where they stood, they witnessed an altercation between a man and a woman. Lamech stood in the shadow of a fork in a tree. Rachel, who always stood closest to Lamech, stood on the other side of the fork. Enos, on the other hand, chose his own shadow to stand in.

When Gerard Pinchuck shoved his wife, he nearly knocked her to the ground. When he walked away, he showed no remorse. He never even looked back. Clearly, she was suffering. Petra would be better off without Gerard. This man would not be missed for long.

Enos looked to Lamech. "Will we be partaking of the man?"

"No. Let the pig wallow."

Rachel was awestruck. In that brief moment, Lamech had once again revealed wisdom that rivaled any she had ever known.

Petra made her way across the street. She was crying again, like she had done so many times before, when she had disappointed her precious man. She hated herself so much that she couldn't bring herself to lift her eyes to the beauty that surrounded her. She was not worthy.

When she reached the block where they stood, they converged on her from three different directions. Rachel and Enos placed their hands on her shoulders. Lamech laid his hand upon her chest. She felt the sub-zero coldness burning into her flesh. She found the will to gaze up where Lamech's face should have been. She stared into the darkness she found there. Just as Lamech had surprised Rachel with his decision, Petra now surprised all three of them with her reaction.

There was no fear. There was no panic. There wasn't even any regret.

"Thank you." She said meekly.

They drew close to her, so close that the four individuals were no longer discernible. When they stepped back, Petra no longer existed. They stood there looking down at the dust on the sidewalk that used to be Petra. Lamech, who had been free of most emotions for many centuries, felt something remarkable to sadness. A life wasted, regardless of the life form, equaled lost potential.

"Since I could not take the time for death..." Enos said.

"Death kindly stopped for me. Emily Dickinson." Lamech finished the quote.

"Race you to Crescent City."

"No, Rachel. We'll sleep here today. Sleep."

"Okay, but first..." Rachel walked over to a fire hydrant and touched the four large bolts at the base of the plug. The next morning, during the heat of rush hour, the pressure of water would send the hydrant sailing in the air. The intersection would become flooded. There would be chaos.

10

When sleep returned this time, it was peaceful and dreamless. HBO continued to bathe multi-colored lights across Peter's eyelids, but rather than distracting him, the colors lulled him. The nice, warm bed was a great contrast to Crescent City's cold breeze that blew outside.

He would have been content to sleep his life away in his own little sequel to the story of Rip Van Winkle, but Marty had other plans in mind for him. When he regained his sense of awareness at last, he could tell by the urgency of her rapping that she had been standing outside for a while. What had felt like mere minutes of sleep, had actually been two hours.

He tramped to the door. With eyes half shut, he felt around the wooden doorjamb until he found the knob for the deadbolt. One flip of his wrist threw the bolt back in its place in the door. A twist of the doorknob caused the door to open a crack. Having done that, he turned around and half staggered, half stumbled his way back to the bed. When his knee bumped the mattress, he flopped face-first back into bed, without saying a word to Marty.

She showed herself to the under-sized chair and table that separated the two beds from the window. She sat and waited, wondering how long she would have to wait for the two detectives to finally wake up. She didn't have to wonder for long.

Peter raised an eyebrow in her direction. "Don't you ever sleep?"

"Probably never again, Sir."

He sat up and took a good look at her. Once again she was immaculately dressed for business. She sat quietly, with her hands folded and resting between her thighs. He wasn't certain if the television was playing tricks with the lighting, but her face was void of expression and had taken on an ashened complexion. He had seen that face on several accident victims, just before they succumbed to shock.

He tossed a pillow at Clark. There was life over there, but only minimal amounts of movement. Peter turned his full attention to Marty. "Are you okay?"

"No. I don't think so, Sir." Marty felt tears welling up. She tried hard to choke back any emotion in her words. "How did you know?"

"I'm sorry, but I'm not sure what your talking about."

"How did you know what I would find?"

Clark sat up, and after surmising the situation, got out of bed and fetched a glass of water for Marty.

"To be honest, I still haven't got a clue of what you are talking about." Peter wished she would get to the point.

Marty stood up and walked to the door. For a moment, Peter thought she was getting ready to storm out, but then he realized that she was hiding her face in the corner. He hadn't known her for more than a day or two, but he knew she wasn't easily given to emotional outbursts. He wondered to himself what could possibly upset her so deeply. Clark stood by the TV, still holding the cup of water.

Marty wiped the tears from her cheeks with her fingers and then tugged at the hem of her jacket. Once she felt she was sufficiently composed enough, she turned to face the guys. Clark sat the cup of water down on the dresser. He took her by the hand and led her to the bed.

"Go ahead. Have a seat." He said, retrieving the cup and handing it to her.

Peter and Clark hunkered down in front of her and waited for her to drink the cup.

"Marty, it's important that we, Clark and I." Peter motioned with his hand to his partner and then to himself. "we need to be caught up to where you are."

"Start from the beginning." Clark added. "Take your time."

Marty wrapped her fingers neatly around the cup and rested it in her lap. She kept her eyes focused on her knees. She started to speak, but there was a quivering in her voice that threatened to choke her. She stopped in mid-sentence. They waited for her to recompose herself.

"I was leaving the station. Captain Stockton came to me. We have two all-night grocery stores, three gas stations, and several bars and nightclubs. He's gotten complaints from the owners. They said that the curfew is going to affect their livelihood."

"More than they know." Peter breathed.

"See? Like that!" She shoved at Peter's shoulder. He almost toppled over on his butt. "How do you know that?"

"It's just a hunch." Clark said in his partner's defense.

"First, Jones hears a noise that should have been impossible for him to detect. He's missing. And now, you know more than you're letting on. Are you going to come up missing next? Is Clark? Am I?"

"No." Peter was adamant.

"It's just a hunch." Clark repeated, but this time it was to convince himself.

"I have hunches too, you know. I went to the prison. Other than the usual riots, it was a complete dead end. No prison breaks. No madman on the loose. There's no Satan-worshipping faction in town—Well, if there is, it's not known to any of my contacts. That was one of my hunches, too. Remember? But you, your hunches..."

"What did you find out?" Peter didn't like where this conversation was heading.

"I talked to a lady, Darla Lovesyou. She's the Yurok equivalence to a shaman or a medicine woman. She told me about a society of demons. Each Native American Nation has their own version of the Devil. They refer to him as the Trickster. But the Yuroks' version is a society of Indian devils, or tricksters. Wait a minute, I have the name written down."

Marty fumbled around in the breast pocket of her jacket. She was visibly shaken. Her hands trembled as she opened her notepad.

"They're called Umai. They look like men, or at least the shadow of men, but if you shine a light directly at them, they vanish." Marty paused to take a breath and steel herself for the next part. "According to legend, they roam the nights looking for souls to steal. If they catch you, they take your soul and replace it with an evil one."

She folded her notepad and strained to not let her nervousness show, as she replaced the notepad back in her pocket. First, she looked at Peter. He was deep in thought and did not make eye contact with her. So she turned to Clark.

"Our perps aren't just stealing souls. They're taking the whole person." Clark said. "That's good news. It proves that we're not dealing with ghosts or goblins. We're dealing with real people just trying to make everyone believe that the supernatural is involved."

"How do you figure?" Marty was incredulous.

"If these legends were real, we would have a bunch of possessed people wandering around, right? Technically, Missing Persons wouldn't have a case. But since these are real people, they have no way of pulling off a hoax like possessed victims. So they're kidnapping these guys. So it's a real possibility that the little boy, Jones, and the security guard are still alive. They're just stowed away somewhere. Just for the record, I don't believe in the supernatural anyhow."

"No. Neither do I." Peter lied. Marty and Clark knew that he was lying, but they chose not to challenge him.

Marty declined to give her opinion.

"Thanks, Marty. If you want, you can go get some rest. Clark and I can handle it for now."

"No, Sir. I'm fine. I need to see this through." Marty looked down at the ground, so she wouldn't have to see their reaction. "Besides, I'd prefer not to be alone for the time being."

"Okay, I understand."

On the carpet of her little living room, she poured a circle of white ash. At the four corners of the circle, she placed a handful of dirt to represent earth, eagle feathers to represent wind, black ashes from the fireplace to represent fire, and a coffee cup full of water, respectfully. Along the white line, she placed an assortment of amulets for luck and protection. Each amulet was evenly spaced. When she had accomplished that, she stood in the center and looked around the room. Nothing was missing. Nothing was out of place. No one was there. She stripped off all of her clothes and laid on her back, naked, in the center of the circle.

"Gods of this world. I lay here, humbled. Watch over me. Protect me. Guide me."

Darla waited for the visions to come. Instead of guidance, she saw the face of a man. He was handsome. In this life, he was known as a searcher of lost children. He was a Protector and a Warrior. His hands were strong. His arms were strong. His mind and heart were strong. She touched herself. Her hands, caressing, were no longer hers. They belonged to the man in the vision.

When the orgasms had subsided, she felt a calm that could only be described as spiritual. Her body was bathed in her own perspiration. Hours had passed since she had entered the circle. The fire in the fireplace had died, and the air had turned cold. Her clothes were outside of the circle. Instead of dressing, she reached for a sheet that covered the couch, without stepping outside the circle. Covering herself with the sheet, she laid down again. She thought of the man's face in the vision. This time, his face brought her sleep.

As she slept, a lone dark figure walked out of her unlighted bathroom. He stopped short of the white circle. His toes were not quite touching the white ash.

He stood there staring at the sleeping woman. She was beautiful, even by his standards. He studied the curve of her face and the roundness of her bare shoulders. His eyes followed the length of her body. The sheet, she used to cover herself, was light enough that it hid precious little of her naked form.

He looked down at the white powdered circle. He could not cross it. She was inaccessible, for the moment.

She was powerful, indeed. This could present a problem. She would be a formidable adversary.

11

"The heroine made her way to A street. From where she was standing, it looked as if the streetlights trailed off into the ocean. She preferred to walk on the macadam-plated road, rather than the sidewalk that dipped at each driveway. The lighthouse was fully illuminated. The gentle bellow of the foghorn announced the forthcoming of a fog bank. The fog was creeping in like a slow straddling guest at a formal ball.

"The closer the heroine came to the end of A street, the more apparent the fog became. It sat on the ocean, like a spider on a web, crawling slowly to the web's edge. The fog would reach the shore in an hour or so.

"The heroine thought of returning home. For the first time since she left the house, she noticed the darkness. She really, really noticed the darkness. She was alone. She was utterly, utterly alone. There was hesitation in each footstep. But she thought of the charming hero, and she envisioned his face. She did her best to not think of all those little quirks of his that bothered her so. If there was to be a romantic interlude between them, it would begin tonight.

"Like a ball-bearing being drawn to a magnet... No. That's too fast. Like a crab being drawn to the rotting corpse of a dead sea lion. It sounds gross, but it works. The heroine fought back the fear that threatened to cripple her, and anxiously, but not too anxiously, walked towards the place that held her lover. No, not lover. Soon-to-be-steady boyfriend.

"What a great story. Damn I'm good."

Mary stood in the Lighthouse parking lot. The Jetty was on the other side of the towering rocks on the far side of the parking lot. There were strange shadowy silhouettes of people grouped together at the base of the rocks. The fog was rolling in around them. The city lights reflected off the fog, creating a diminutive back-lighting effect. Mary was expecting to see Roger, Kayla, T-Jack, and Rosie, but there were so many more.

"Mary! There she is! Mary! We're over here!"

Mary recognized Kayla's heavy, bubbly voice. She waved, as she walked towards Kayla. Her eyes scanned the crowd of people for Roger. She spotted him behind a smaller group of people. Either he hadn't noticed her yet, or he was pretending to not notice her. She hated that.

Most of the people there were in their later teens or early twenties. Mary suspected that she was the youngest. The guy that Roger was talking to was older, much older. Mary couldn't be certain how old the man was, but he was probably in his forties or fifties. There was something out of place about this guy. It was quirky. He didn't belong there. Or maybe it was she that didn't belong.

"Dude, you made it. Right on. Hella-cool."

"Thanks, Dude." Mary said, but it sounded corny when she said it. She vowed to herself, to just act natural from now on.

Almost in unison, the group of people headed down the slightly inclined dirt road that led to the Jetty. There was a security gate that kept vehicles from driving out onto the breakwater, but foot traffic climbed over, under, or quite simply enough, walked around the gate. The view was breathtaking, even at night. Maybe it was because of the night that caused the view to be so spectacular. The lighthouse was just off to the right, across a tide pool. The fisherman's dock was off a distance to the left. Across the harbor, Mary could see the lights and dock, where the commercial fishermen parked their boats.

A little further out was the Coast Guard station, though the fog had all but completely obscured it. At the mouth of the harbor, Mary could barely make out the green and red lights that guided the boats around the rocks. And just to the right of that, a single light burned in the tower that housed the foghorn.

"So what exactly am I looking at?" With the exception of the lights, Mary couldn't see more than fifty yards down the Jetty. The fog had become a pea-soup monster that gobbled up the rest of the breakwater.

"What do you mean?" Kayla said.

Mary had seen the Jetty once in the daylight. She knew that it was L-shaped. She knew of the foghorn tower that was on the other end of the L. She knew that the L formed the right side of the harbor. That was all that she knew.

"What exactly is a Jetty?"

"Oh, this is nothing. You ought to see it on a clear night, when the tide is in and the waves are crashing over the top."

"That can happen?"

"Yeah, sure. All the time. But we're in luck tonight. The tide will stay out for a few more hours."

"We should be fine." T-Jack joined in. "Unless, of course, there's a Tsunami."

"Wait a minute, What's a Tsunami?" This was becoming a worse idea with each passing minute.

"It's another word for a tidal wave." Since T-Jack was the Brains of the group, this was his opportunity to dominate the conversation.

"Is that why they built the Jetty? to protect the town from Tsunamis?" Mary loved to dig for facts. One never knows when a story will pop up.

T-Jack laughed. "Not hardly. The Jetty just keeps the other waves from destroying the commercial boats. Back in 1964, there was an earthquake up in Alaska. It sent four Tsunamis this way. The first one struck town just after midnight. It came all the way in to Second Street. The fourth wave reached all the way to Sixth Street. It killed twelve people. On its way in, it picked up one of the tetrapods out here..." He pointed towards the Jetty. "Well you can't see them from here. I'll show you one when we get to it. But the Tsunami picked up a tetrapod and carried the tetrapod all the way in to Front Street."

"Oh." Mary said.

T-Jack realized that Mary wasn't impressed, so he added. "These tetrapods weigh at least twenty-five tons."

"Oh!" Mary repeated herself, but this time with more emotion.

"Ooh. Someone was actually paying attention in History." Kayla teased.

"Hey, that's what I do. Anyways, Mary. That tetrapod is still there. They built a monument around it. Maybe I can show it to you someday."

"I would like that." Mary walked over to the edge of the Jetty and peered down. The ocean was twelve feet below. The swells were only three feet high, but they still made an impressive splash.

"There aren't any rails here. What if someone falls over?"

"It happens, but you would have to be a complete ninny. Maybe you better come stand over here." Kayla said, jokingly.

When they had walked for what seemed to Mary to be a mile, they came to the end of the first leg of the L-shaped Jetty. Their path was impeded by piles of tetrapods. With the harbor to her back, she could not see the ocean— the tetrapods were so large, and there were so many of them. When a wave came in, the water filled into caverns created by the way the tetrapods were stacked. The fanfare of the ocean made conversation difficult.

"What is this area?" Mary shouted, referring to the circular section they were standing on.

"This is the helipad for the Coast Guards." Kayla shouted back.

After hearing expressions such as hella-lame, hella-cool, hella-this, and hella-that, the word helipad struck Mary as amusing. She had a feeling it was a helipad, before she had asked. It was reassuring to know she was right, though she couldn't figure out what difference it made.

Someone opened a twelve-pack of beer. Mary declined when Kayla offered her a can. Kayla lit a cigarette and offered Mary one. Mary declined this also. After the third person in ten minutes offered her a beer, she finally accepted one. Once people saw that she was carrying a can, they stopped bugging her. They failed to notice that she never popped the first one open, but that was okay.

She surveyed around the area. She didn't see Roger anywhere. She spotted the older man standing by one of the enormous tetrapods. He appeared to be flirting with Rosie. "God, what a sleaze." Mary said, not loud enough to be heard above the ocean's din. Rosie didn't seem to mind the attention, so Mary decided to leave it alone.

Instead, she tugged at Kayla's coat sleeve. "Did you see where Roger went to?"

"Naw, he's probably out there, somewhere." Kayla pointed to the place everyone was calling the maze. "He's smoking a bowl, I'll bet. Dude, you want some?"

Mary shook her head, disdainfully. She mentally added one more item to the list of Roger's quirks. His shining armor was becoming more tarnished, indeed.

"Okay, here's the deal. Once you enter the Maze, you have to stay on the tetrapods. If you step on the flat surface, you're out."

"What happens if you fall into the water?"

"Dude, you're dead."

Mary didn't like the sound of that. She wondered if there was a tactful way to excuse herself and go back home. Probably not.

Her attention turned to another sound that rose off in the distance. It sounded like a pack of wild dogs with whooping coughs. It seemed like a good idea to make sure that they weren't about to be mauled by wild animals.

"What's that?"

"What's what?" It was apparent that Kayla was getting annoyed with the incessant questions.

"That noise?"

Kayla listened for a moment. "Oh, that. Those are the sea lions over at the docks." Kayla pointed across the harbor. "They do that all night. On a good night, you can hear them all the way across town. You'll get used to it. You ready?"

"I've never seen a sea lion. Let's do that instead."

"Dude, it's a federal offense to mess with sea lions. You're not afraid, are you?"

"I'm not afraid of anything." Mary said, then she added just under her breath. "There's just a few things I don't like."

Kayla ran up to a redheaded guy with thick glasses. She grabbed him by the shoulders and shouted. "Okay everybody. Arnie's it."

The guy who was obviously Arnie jerked away from Kayla's grasp. "Oh come on. I'm always it."

"No, you're not."

"Yes, I am."

"Dude, just do it this time and you won't have to again. I promise."

Arnie slumped his shoulders. "I've heard that before." He muttered.

Kayla lit another cigarette and blew out a long plume of smoke. She reached out with the lit cigarette. Instinctively, Mary reached out to take it, but then she shook her head.

"Dude, you don't do anything, do you?"

The question didn't seem to warrant an answer, so Mary remained silent.

"I'm only counting to a hundred, this time." Arnie shouted. "One. Two. Three..."

The gang scattered towards the semi-circle of tetrapods. Mary paused to gaze at these eerie sentries that guarded against the ocean. Their sharp angles stood out against the fog, reminding Mary of a thorn patch in a Disney cartoon.

Kayla took Mary by the hand. "Come on." She led Mary through the mouth of the Maze, before she finally let go.

Mary found herself alone. She climbed up on one of the tetrapods and dropped down on to another, on the other side. She continued this course until she came to a dead end. The pods ahead were too high to climb. She couldn't see below the pods, into the dark recesses there, but she could hear the waves washing in below her. Going under was not an option, so she sat down and waited to see what would happen next.

After a while, Mary's eyes became accustomed to the dark. She saw that she was not as alone as she thought she was. There were two figures in the dark, a short distance away. Mary stared at the them until her eyes focused. It was Rosie and that creepy old guy, and they were kissing. Mary felt nausea crawling into her stomach. She kept low and began retracing her steps. She would rather be "it", than witness what she had just seen. By backtracking her path, she found her way back to the main corridor. She recognized the graffiti that showed the way out. When she stepped out on the helipad, she felt that she could breathe again, though in reality the air wasn't any different.

Once again, she thought she was alone, but someone came up behind her and threw his arms around her neck. She screamed, swung her elbow back, and spun out of his grasp.

Roger was standing there, doubled over and holding his stomach.

"Oh, Roger. I'm so sorry. You startled me."

"I was worried about you." Roger gasped. He straightened up, keeping his arms folded across his abdomen. "I hadn't seen you for a while."

"Are you okay?"

"Yeah, sure. You didn't hit me that hard." Roger lied. His face had a wrenched look, as if he was about to vomit.

"You were worried about me? Really?"

"Not any more. Where did you learn that?" Roger rubbed his stomach.

"My father made me and my mom take self-defense classes. I never thought I would be using it on a friend. Are you sure you're all right?"

"I'm fine. I hardly felt a thing." His breathing was still slightly labored. "Hey, come on. I want to show you something." He took her by the hand and led her back into the maze. When he found a dark corner, he looked around to make sure they were alone.

"Well? What did you want to show me?"

"This." Roger gave her a quick kiss on the lips. Since she didn't put up any resistance, he kissed her again. This time he let the kiss linger. When she kissed him back, he slipped his tongue between her lips.

Mary was torn between the emotional, romantic implications and repulsed by the acrid, sour taste and smell that bombarded her senses. She surmised that it must be a combination of beer and marijuana. His kisses became more forceful, more lustful. He unzipped her jacket and slid his hand inside.

When she grabbed his wrist and tried to pull his hand away, he squeezed her breast. She wrestled herself away. Once she was free, she rubbed her sore breast through the jacket.

"I'm sorry." Roger said. "I'll behave myself."

Mary cupped her breasts gingerly, protectively. Roger leaned in and kissed her again. And then he kissed her again. Then he threw an arm around her, pinning her own arms at her side. He used his free hand to unbutton and unzip her jeans.

"No! Don't!" She cried out. He covered her mouth with his own. She tried to wriggle free to no avail. He had her pinned tight.

He slid his hand in under her panties and wedge his fingers between her thighs. She tried to call for help, but every sound was muffled by his own lips. He was attempting to insert one of his fingers. She knew what had to be done. She didn't like it, but he left her no choice.

She brought her knee up into his groin. He yanked his hand away. Because it was too hard to get any leverage when someone has their hand in one's crotch, she grabbed him by the shoulder. "I said, 'No'." She brought her knee up again, this time with more force. Roger fell to the ground and curled up in a ball.

"Oh my God! You bitch!" He wheezed.

Mary ran for the main corridor, zipping and buttoning her pants as she went. Finding her way to the helipad was easier, this time. There were several people standing around. Mary ignored them. She was heading for the shore.

"Mary? What's wrong? Where are you going?"

She recognized Kayla's voice. She paused for a moment, but she was determined to go home, so she started walking again. Kayla caught up with her.

"You can't leave. It's not safe."

"I have to go. Something bad happened."

"What?"

"I don't want to talk about it. Please, I have to go."

"Okay, dude. I'll come with you. Just let me say good-bye to some of the guys, so they don't think we fell in. Okay?"

"Okay, but hurry."

Suddenly, Rosie ran out onto the helipad. "Help me! He's gone!" Everybody converged on Rosie. Mary followed behind.

"Who's gone?" Someone shouted.

"Guy! He just disappeared."

"Did he fall in?" Kayla put her arm around Rosie's shoulder in an attempt to get Rosie to calm down.

"No!   One moment he was there, and then he just disappeared."

"He fell in." Someone else concluded.

"We have to find him!" Rosie said.

"Okay, okay. We'll look for him. But Rosie, dude, you need to calm down." Kayla said. She put her hand on Rosie's head and cradled it against her own shoulder. She released her grip on Rosie's head long enough to light a cigarette. When she had taken a long drag from it, she handed it off to Rosie. Rosie took it, and Kayla lit another for herself.

"What's that?" Mary shouted.

"Dude, it's just the sea lions."

"Not that! That." Mary pointed to the straightway of the Jetty. Just barely visible in the fog were six shadowy figures standing side by side.

"It's Guy." Rosie shouted.

"No, dude. It's the cops." Kayla hissed.

"They can help us find Guy." Rosie broke away from Kayla and ran towards the men in the fog. "Can you help us?" She shouted. "We've lost someone."

Rosie stopped and stood in front of one of the men. She began to back away from that person. As she turned to run away, the man reached out and grabbed her by the wrist.

"It's cold!" She screamed. Instinctively, she pressed the lit end of her cigarette against the man's arm. He burst into a fireball.

Rosie's cigarette fell to the cement top of the Jetty. The flesh of her wrist was severely singed. She held her arm against her chest with her other arm and turned to run back to the safety of the group.

One of the other shadowy figures grabbed her by the shoulders. She winced, then the man stepped into her. But he didn't step into her. It was as if he took her inside of him. They literally became one.

Mary remembered seeing something like this in her biology class. The man was like a phagocyte, and Rosie was a cancerous cell. Mary couldn't be certain in the night's fog, but she would swear she saw dust falling out of the dark figure.

"Run!" Someone shouted.

Mary watched as one of the shadow men jumped into a darkened recess of the tetrapods and appear fifty feet closer. He grabbed a boy, that was scrambling over a tetrapod, and pulled the boy into him. The boy screamed before he vanished.

Kayla grabbed Mary's jacket. "Come on! This way!"

They ran back into the maze. T-Jack was right behind them. They reached the point where Mary had left Roger. He had somehow managed to stand and was making his way to the corridor.

T-Jack spotted Roger and called out to him. "Roger! Come on, man! They're killing everybody!"

"Who is?"

"Those men back there!"

Though he was experiencing some difficulties, Roger picked up his pace. They found their way through the maze. On the back side, there was seventy yards of boulders and then another flat surface that led to the foghorn tower.

As they made their way over the rough terrain, Kayla fell behind. Mary turned to monitor Kayla's progress. She saw a dark figure come out of the maze.

"Run, Kayla, run!" She cried.

Kayla looked up at Mary. The man came up behind her. Mary watched in horror as her friend dissolved into blackness.

"No! Kayla! No!" Mary screamed. She turned towards the harbor, took a moment to look out over the water, then shouted. "Guys! This way! Go into the water!"

She climbed down the rocks to the harbor, where the waves weren't as turbulent. T-Jack was beside her. Roger was coming up close behind.

"We'll die of hypothermia!" Roger shouted.

"We'll die if we don't!" Mary shouted back.

T-Jack dove in. Mary followed. Roger hesitated, but then he jumped in.

When they were together again and swimming towards the lights of the park Mary called out to the other two. "Keep your arms and legs moving. Keep the blood circulating. Use the waves to carry you forward. Are there any sharks in these waters?"

"Yeah, leopard sharks." Roger called back.

"Don't worry. They're bottom-dwellers. They're afraid of humans." T-Jack added.

Mary looked back at the Jetty, where they had entered the water. Three men stood watching. Mary's heart was racing before, but to see the men standing where Mary and the guys were, just moments before, made Mary's heart skip a beat all together.

Her arms and legs were numb. She could feel herself shuddering. Hypothermia was setting in.

A wave came up behind her. She arched her back, raised her arms, and bent her legs at the knees to keep her feet from dragging. When the wave had passed over her, she continued swimming with short, fast strokes, until the next wave came.

They had swam halfway to the park. Mary was leading the way. Roger stopped swimming.

"T-Jack?" Roger called out.

Mary stopped swimming and looked behind her. "What's wrong?"

"T-Jack is missing. He was here a minute ago. What do we do?"

Mary scanned the water. They were alone. "Keep swimming."

"What about T-Jack?"

"We can't help him. Keep swimming."

Mary let a sigh of relief escape, when her foot finally struck bottom. Her foot was numb so she wasn't certain what she felt at first. She'll never forgive her father for making her watch those Jaws movies. She stood up and waded to the beach. Roger caught up with her.

"We made it! We escaped." Roger exclaimed, as he flopped down on the sand by Mary's feet.

"We didn't escape. They let us go."

"How do you know that?"

"I saw them. They watched us swim away."

Roger raised himself up on his hands and knees and vomited on the sand. When the lurching in his stomach had subsided, he turned over and sat down. He used his wet sleeve to wipe off his mouth.

Mary sat down beside him and looked out towards the foghorn. She was hoping that T-Jack would rise up out of the surf. Somehow, she knew he wouldn't.

She looked over at Roger. His trembling was synchronous to her own shivering. Despite her new-found contempt for him, she was relieved that he had survived.

"We have to get out of these wet clothes. But if you do anything that is less than gentlemanly, I'll have you on the ground again."

"Don't worry. I've learned my lesson. Besides, you're not my type."

"I'll bet I'm not."

Mary looked back at the ocean, again. The tide was on its way in.

"How far was that?"

Roger looked back in the direction of her gaze. "A little short of a mile. Why?" He said.

"Just curious. Remind me to tell my mother that it's definitely too cold to go swimming."

"Yeah. If we don't freeze to death first."

12

By the time they headed for the conference room of the small police station, they had rehashed every angle of ever possibility of every scenario of every scheme of every criminal mind. Or so they thought. Their main intention at the time was to cross-reference all known files of all the known perps in the area, preferably with Yurok heritage. Someone, or someones, were going through a lot of trouble to imitate a Yurok legend. The answer was simple — Find the people that would benefit from such a hoax, and single out any criminal that would be capable of pulling off such a hoax.

Without saying as much, Clark was relieved that the attention was taken away from the supernatural. He could concentrate on the natural and the tangible. Now, they would make some progress.

They were prepared to read each file and compare it with all the other files, until they had at least six to nine persons closely associated with each other. Six to nine perps that would fit the profiles. Once they had this list, they would start the interrogating process, until at least one suspect cracked. They were prepared to carry the investigation all the way up to the Yurok Council, if needed.

Once they reached the little cobblestone building that housed the Police Department, they found the place buzzing with activity. The streets were lined with privately owned vehicles, some of which were abandoned in such haste that the headlights were left on. Squad cars accented the scene with red, white, and blue dome lights flashing.

A crowd of people were forced to stand outside, on the sidewalk. The lobby, which Peter had thought was too small anyway, was filled beyond the fire code capacity.

"What do we do now?" Peter turned to Marty.

"This way." Marty called out to Peter and Clark. "We'll use the service entrance."

They ran around to the side of the building. Marty fumbled around with a set of keys until she found the one for that door. Before she slid the key into the lock, she looked around to make sure the mob hadn't followed. She pulled the door open and held it as the two gentlemen went through. Once she was inside, she let the heavy door swing shut, then gave it a reassuring tug to make sure it had latched properly.

Captain Stockton, who had been at home eating dinner with his wife when the reports started pouring in, was sitting at his desk. He was disturbed from his office the moment he heard the service door open. He was relieved to see Marty and the Detectives.

"Captain, what's going on?" Marty had been leading the way down the hall when the Captain stepped out of his office.

"Step this way. I need you guys to update me on your case."

Once they had filed into his office and were seated before his desk, it took them all of fifteen minutes to bring the Captain up to par. The Captain exchanged with them about the commotion out in the lobby. Apparently, ten or more teenagers had violated the curfew. It was suspected that they were partying together. The exact location had not yet been determined. Several of the known favorite sites had been searched, but as yet, nothing had turned up.

"Where have they looked, so far?" Marty said.

We have a team out on Pleasant grove. One team out at Point St. George, doing a foot search. And a team up at the lookout, doing a foot search of the trails. When they're finished there, they'll make their way to the harbor." The Captain paused for a moment, then added, "It's already too late, isn't it."

Peter didn't think it was possible for the Captain to look any more solemn, but he did.

"There isn't anything else for you here, Sir. Go home to your wife." Marty said.

"Have you got any ideas, Marty?"

"Maybe, Sir. We'll call you if we find anything, Sir."

"We're on top of it, Captain. We'll get these guys." Clark said.

"Go home to your wife. You should be with her now, Sir."

"She's been under a lot of stress, lately." Captain Stockton offered as an explanation to the two detectives. "You will call me as soon as you find out anything?"

"The very first thing, Sir." Marty was out the door before the other two had even stood up. Peter jumped up and followed. When Clark was left behind, he looked at the Captain, gave a quick shrug, then he jumped up and ran after Marty and Peter.

When Clark caught up to Peter, he said, "So much for the curfew."

"I told you it was a bad idea."

"Don't even try it. That was your idea."

"Marty." Peter called out to her. "Wasn't the curfew, Clark's idea?"

"I'm not at liberty to say, Sir." Marty was still leading the way towards the service door.

"See? I told you." Peter said to Clark.

"What? See what? Hey, Marty!"

The Gold-colored Cadillac made its way to the lighthouse at Marty's suggestion. When Peter had parked the car and climbed out, he was taken back by the beauty of it all. With the fog enveloping the lighthouse, the scene reminded him of some movie he had seen along time ago. Everything was so romantic, nostalgic, sad, and haunting.

Marty was standing in front of the car. When Peter and Clark joined her, she pointed off in the distance. "That's where I last saw Jones."

"Marty, is that why you brought us here?" Clark asked, sympathetically.

"No. I'm sorry. It's just that... Well, he was a good person. We just had personality clashes."

"I understand. I do." Clark said. "What is it that you want to show us?"

Peter noted that there wasn't any other cars in the parking lot, but that didn't dissuade Marty. Marty led them down the path that led to the Jetty. With flashlights and handguns drawn, they made their way around the security gate.

"Oh, no. This is not good." Marty said.

"What's not good?" Peter turned to see what she was referring to.

"Well, it's kind of hard to tell in this fog, but I think the tide is coming in. We'll have to hurry."

"Just exactly how far are we going?" Clark tried to peer into the fog. He couldn't see the end of this breakwater that everyone called the Jetty. He seemed to recall from his previous visits to Crescent City, that it was quite a distance.

"It's about three-quarters of a mile, Sir. We need to hurry."

Though time was crucial, their travel was impeded by the dark, the fog, and the kelp that partially covered the Jetty's cement surface. In several places, miniature tidepools were being formed in the cement deck, from years of erosion. Even though the Jetty was wide enough to drive a dump truck on it, there was no guardrails along the sides. If a person wasn't paying attention, they could stumble off the side.

"The tide is definitely coming in. We have to move faster. You don't want to be out here at high tide."

"What happens at high tide?" Clark was beginning to trail behind.

"Well, it's not even high tide. When the tide is coming in, The waves washes over the Jetty with enough force to knock anyone standing on it out into the water."

"Good point. Important point. Thank you for bringing it up...Now! Hey Pete! Did you hear her?"

"Yes. So we probably should hurry, don't you think?" Peter shouted over his shoulder.

It took them a total of forty-five minutes to reach the helipad at the end of the first leg. There were so many potholes and slippery spots. Every twenty yards or so, they shined their lights over the side, to see if there was any sign of life. Nothing was moving but the waves and the crabs that climbed on the rocks below. When they finally made it to the helipad, Marty ran into the mouth of the maze. Clark, on the other hand, took a more direct approach — He climbed over one of the groupings of tetrapods. Peter stayed behind to investigate the perimeter of the helipad.

Several minutes had passed before Marty reemerged from the maze. "There's nobody here. I don't understand it. I was so sure they would be."

Clark appeared over the top of one of the pods. It was a four-foot drop to the deck of the helipad. "Man, oh, man. That was scary. You've got the water gushing in under you. You have to watch where you step. There's dead ends, everywhere. I got lost. Hey, Pete. You should try this."

Peter was kneeling down examining a pile of what appeared to be a powder. He couldn't be certain by the illumination of the flashlight, but the powder appeared to be reddish-pink. His first impression was that it was some kind of new drug. He laughed that idea out of his head. There was way too much of it to be any kind of a drug. There were piles of it everywhere.

"There's nobody here." Marty shouted above the roar of the waves, to Clark.

"If they had been here, they're gone now." He added.

Peter stood up. "They were here all right. Most of the beer cans around here, aren't opened. Have you ever known a party to leave this much beer behind?"

"No. You're right." Clark said.

"Look at this." Peter pointed to the pile of powder on the deck. "Tell me what you think of it."

"Jeez. What is it?" Clark said after he had taken a moment to analyze the powder.

"I don't know, but it is everywhere. Look around."

Clark could see that his partner was right. Everywhere he looked there were piles of the powder, even on the tetrapods. It occurred to him that he had just been up there. He looked down. He had the dust on his hands. It was on his clothing.

"Excuse me, Peter? Clark? Sirs? We should be going soon."

Peter looked at Clark. "Do you have any of those little specimen bags?"

"No. Do you?"

"No. Marty?"

"I'm so sorry, Sir. I wasn't planning on... I'm sorry."

They made another sweep of the area. There was no one else. Anyone that attended the party had been surgically removed.

It was 3 am. Even at high tide, the helipad usually stayed dry. They hadn't realized that waves were already washing over the Jetty, until then.

"Oh my God! We're too late!" Marty cried out.

Peter and Clark looked back at the shore in time to see a spray completely sweep across the deck. They tracked the wave as it traveled the length of the Jetty, until the wave was lost in the fog.

"This can't be good." Peter said out loud. Then he turned to Marty. "Options?"

"We stay here for three hours and hope the ocean calms down. Or we take our chances with the waves." Marty explained.

"We don't have three hours to waste."

"Okay. This is what you do. First, no running. You'll slip and fall, and crack your head open. That will be the end. Second, stay to the left. Each of the waves are going to splash up on the deck. Most of them, we should be able to take standing, but every sixth or seventh wave is a big one. When that one hits drop to your stomach, hold your breath, and hang on to the side. If you lose your grip, the wave should be finished before you actually slide off the other side." Marty said, as she pointed to the different areas for emphasis.

"This is a good suit." Clark complained. "I really love this suit."

Peter patted him on the shoulder. "I'll see to it that your buried in it."

"You think you're funny. You're not funny. I know funny, and you're not it."

"Are you guys ready? Wait for my count and follow my lead."

Marty waited until she saw the spray then, in spite of her own warning, took off running. Peter and Clark stayed as close as they could. Marty carefully kept track of the path ahead of her, while keeping an eye on the ocean to her left. If she ran off the edge, a broken leg that she would surely sustain, would be the least of her troubles. Peter almost plowed into her, the first time she crouched. Clark just barely squatted, when the wave hit them from the side.

"Shit! That's cold!" He shouted, but the other two were already up and running.

Peter was impressed at how far they had traveled, before the first wave hit them, but now their progress was taking a slower pace. The freshly hydrated seaweed and lichen that grew on the Jetty, left little to be desired in regards of traction.

He was keeping a closer eye on Marty. He didn't want to trip over her, as he had almost did the first time. This time, when she looked to her left, she didn't just merely squat. Marty threw herself down in a prone position and grabbed the edge of the breakwater. Instincts dictated to Peter to follow her gaze. What he saw took his breath away. Though visibility was poor, there was something about watching a wave as it built up momentum, bristled with trapped energy, and waiting to release that energy on anything in it's path that caused a person to pause. He dove for the deck of the Jetty.

Clark didn't get the message until the wave was upon him. It threw him down across Peter's legs. Clark flailed his arms until he found Peter's ankle. He held on tight and prayed that Peter's grip was strong enough to hold them both.

When the icy water had settled, they were up again. Thirty seconds later, they were down on their hands and knees again. When this wave hit, it sent Marty sprawling on her stomach. Peter reached out and grabbed her wrist, but the combined magnitude of her weight and the force of the wave pulled him to his stomach, also. He dropped the toes of one of his foot over the edge and used it as an anchor.

When that wave had passed, they were up and moving once again. Clark realized that his suit jacket, now that it was thoroughly drenched, was doing nothing to keep him warm and creating a hindrance. When he pulled it off and threw it down, his flashlight fell out of the pocket and clattered away. He turned back to retrieve the flash light. Peter yelled for him to forget it. He thought about taking off his shoulder holster and service revolver and discarding them as well, but then he thought better of it.

Peter skinned out of his soaked jacket, as well. He noticed that the closer they had gotten to land, the less force there was in the waves. After a while, even the sixth wave was more of an annoyance, than an actual threat.

Marty crouched down and vomited saltwater. When her stomach had finally stopped bucking, she stood up. Peter and Clark grabbed her by each of her arms, and they ran until they reached the shoreline. Their fingers were stiff from the cold. Pain shot up their arms and legs. They were dangerously close to hypothermia.

When they reached the car, Clark climbed in the back seat. Peter pulled a couple of wool blankets out of the trunk and handed them to Clark to wrap up in. Peter climbed into the driver's seat, turned the engine over, and turned the heater on high.

"Can you believe some people do what we just did, for the fun of it?" Marty said.

"No, thank you." Clark said.

"You won't catch me out there." Peter added. "We better get back to the hotel and change. Marty. I have a set of sweats that should fit you."

"Thank you, sir."

"You're welcome. And please stop calling me Sir."

"Thank you, Peter. Sir."

13

"The heroine looked over at the man who was the former object of her affection. She saw him for what he was. No longer was he a knight in shining armor, but he was a slimy banana slug in a tin can. Yet the heroine, with all of her good qualities, could not allow him to die. She would have to save him for the Authorities. They would know how to handle this low life and his parasitic needs. Damn, I'm good."

"What? Did you say something?"

"No. I was just thinking out loud." Mary replied.

It took awhile for Roger's Bic lighter to dry out enough to emit a flame. They had gathered some driftwood from the beach. Mary grabbed a handful of pine needles and brought it to the barbecue pit. She dug through a garbage-can until she found some paper plates and napkins. She piled up the paper products and lit the pile. When the fire was out of danger of being smothered, she sprinkled the pine needles on the pile. Once the needles had ignited, she began laying twigs on the flames, then small sticks. Soon she had an impressive pyre burning.

She didn't like parading around in her panties and bra, but for the moment it was an undesirable necessity. She could feel Roger's watchful eyes upon her the whole time. He was smart enough to keep his distance.

It had been hours since they emerged from the water. The sun would be rising in a couple of hours. Her father told her, once, that the coldest time of the day was the last couple of hours before the sun rose. She knew he was right.

They had wrung out their clothes several times, but the clothes were still too damp to put on. Roger occupied his time by holding each item of clothing in front of the fire. After a short period, he switched the articles of clothing. This proved to be an ineffective way of drying clothes, but Mary didn't care. It kept Roger occupied.

Mary kept her blood circulating by hopping around. Occasionally, She would come close to the fire, warming both sides, and then she would continue to hop. Roger never ventured more than a few feet away from the fire.

"Maybe we should... I've heard that the best way to conserve body heat is to... Don't you think we ought to...?"

Mary stopped hopping. She did her best Bruce Lee stance. Her feet were slightly more than shoulder width apart. She bent her knees slightly. She held one arm in front for defense. The other arm was up and back behind her head, ready to strike. She waved him toward her.

"You want it? Come and get it."

"Forget it. I hope you freeze."

Mary hated to admit it, but she was having fun. She almost forgot the strange people on the Jetty, when she saw how miserable Roger was. Mary started hopping again. Her blood pressure was up. She was breathing heavy. In spite of the cold, she could feel beads of sweat forming on her forehead. She kept a watchful eye toward the darkness. When her bouncing brought her close to the fire, she made a quick check to ensure that there were plenty of sticks poking out of the fire. She paused long enough to warm herself by the fire, then she was off again.

"Hey. Roger. Since. You're. Just. Sitting. There. Any. Ways. Why. Don't. You. Check. The. Clothes. And. See. If. They. Are. Dry."

"Check them yourself."

"Aww. Don't. Be. Mean. If. You. Check. Them. I'll. Give. You. A. Kiss."

"Really?"

"No." Mary stopped hopping. "What's that?"

Roger's face paled. "What's what?"

"There!" She said, pointing in the direction of the water treatment plant. "A car!" She ran over to the fire and grabbed a stick. She took off running in the direction of the car, with her torch held high above her head.

"Mary! Wait! Don't leave me!" Roger stayed for only a moment. Within seconds, he was right behind her with his own make shift torch in hand. They waved frantically and yelled, as they ran toward what appeared to be a golden luxury car.

Peter turned the car down around the water treatment plant. Something told him to take a quick look around the beach and the park. He was sure that they wouldn't find anything, yet there was that nagging feeling that wouldn't leave him.

They had only been in the car for a few minutes, when Marty shouted. "Peter, stop! Stop the car!"

Peter slammed on the brakes. Marty was out of the car before it came to a complete stop. Clark popped out of the back seat. His revolver was drawn, though he had no idea what was going on.

Peter climbed out of the car. His own service revolver was drawn and held off to his side. He kept his gun pointed at the ground. He trailed Marty down a small incline and through the tree line.

When he ran out on the soccer field, he saw what had alerted Marty. Two Teenagers, dressed only in their underwear, were running toward them. Marty must have seen the torches the young couple were carrying. They reached the girl first. The young man was close behind.

"You have to get us out of here!" The girl demanded frantically.

"Where are your clothes?" Marty said.

"They're back by the fire. Leave them. We have to get out of here."

Peter guarded the perimeter. His gun pointed out into the darkness. The streetlights, on the other side of the park, revealed nothing.

"Were you two with a larger group, earlier?" Marty probed.

"They're gone. They're all gone. We're the only two left."

Clark reached the other four. He took a stance opposite of Peter. His own weapon was pointed in another area of emptiness. He had no idea what he was looking for, but he remained ready for anything.

"What do you mean they're gone?" Marty continued her interrogation.

"You won't believe me."

"Try us."

"These people came out of the darkness and made them disappear."

"Why didn't they take you? How did you manage to escape?"

"We jumped into the water and swam across the harbor."

"Are you serious? That's at least a mile in freezing water." Marty looked over at the young man. He nodded his head. "Peter! Clark! We have to get these kids out of here."

Without any delays, they ran toward the car. Peter and Clark held their positions on both flanks. They continued their watch until everyone was inside the car.

Peter grabbed the mike and informed the station that they had located two of the missing Teenagers. The officer on the other end of the line promised to have two people waiting at the back entrance. It would have been chaos trying to get the young couple in through the front door. Once they deposited the kids, Peter drove straight to the hotel.

Captain Stockton hadn't been home for more than an hour. After polishing off a chicken drumstick and a glass of milk from the refrigerator, he climbed the stairs to the bedroom. He slipped between the covers and gave his wife a hug. Sleep was creeping in. The bed felt warm and safe in comparison to the rest of the world. Comforting sleep would be good.

Margot woke with a start. "Honey, someone's outside."

"So let them stay outside." Captain Stockton said through a cloud of exhaustion.

"It's a burglar."

"All the more reason to keep him outside."

"Aren't you going to go investigate?"

"No."

"Hey, young man. How are we going to make this marriage work if I have to do all the work?"

"Mar, for Christ's sake, we've been together for twenty-seven years. What makes you think I want this marriage to work? Now go back to sleep and let the burglar work in peace."

Captain Stockton was feeling sleep take over, again. He was hardly conscious when his wife squirmed out of his grasp. Only his subconscience registered his wife's muttering, as she put on her housecoat. She walked out of the bedroom and descended the staircase.

His eyes sprung open when he heard his wife unlock the front door. "Margot! No!" He leaped out of bed and took the stairs, two at a time.

Margot was standing in the entrance. The door was wide open. Her attention was focused on something in the front yard.

She called out to someone. "What do you think you're doing?"

There was no answer.

"Do you know who my husband is?"

Still no answer.

The Captain had reached the first landing. "No, Margot! Get away from the door!" He could see beyond his wife, now. He saw six men standing in the darkness. One man was climbing the steps of the porch. The others were drawing closer, cutting across the lawn.

"That's right, Mister. Come on up here, so I can see who you are." Margot said.

Stockton leaped. He hit the floor, running. When he reached his wife, he wrapped one arm around her waist. He used his free hand to throw the door shut. Knowing he wouldn't have time to lock it, he threw his weight against the door. With his wife still in tow, he slid to the floor. Margot settled into his lap.

He looked up at the deadbolt and his heart skipped a beat. A shadowy hand protruded the crack in the doorjamb. The fingers splayed, balled into a fist, splayed again, then effortlessly pulled back until it had vanished beyond the door.

The doorbell rang.

"Do you want me to answer that?"

14

Marty was the first to use the shower. Peter's sweats were two sizes larger than the ones that Marty usually wore. Since Clark was stockier than Peter, she had to make due with Peter's outfit. Peter didn't want to be disrespectful by staring, but he had to admit to himself that Marty looked good in his clothes. It was obvious that she was not wearing any underwear under the sweats. She wasn't at all comfortable, and Peter felt himself blushing everytime they made eye contact.

A call from headquarters informed them that the Coast Guard helicopter had been dispatched, along with several boats and foot patrol. As of yet, there had been no sign of any other survivors. No bodies were found.

At the request of Peter, Marty made a phone call to her Native American contact. After Marty's conversation with the woman last evening and the events that had just taken place, Peter was sure the woman could shed more light on the situation. If they were going to battle these shadow-people, real or imagined, they were going to need more information. This Darla Lovesyou was the one who held the answers.

"Darla. I'm so sorry to wake you." Marty said to the receiver of the hotel room's phone. "Yes, I know it's still early. Uh-huh. Yes, I agree. It is an inconvenience. But if you could come down to the station, we would like to ask you some more questions. As soon as possible. If you could, we would be very greatful. Thank-you, Darla. You don't know how important this is. You do? How? Right, of course. Two hours will be fine. I'm sorry for waking you. Thank-you."

When Marty replaced the receiver, she look around the room. She could tell that Peter and Clark had been listening to her side of the conversation. It was annoying that they weren't as surprised as she.

"What do they teach you in detective school.?"

"Not this." Peter said. "This is different."

"Yeah, this is just a hunch." Clark added.

Mary and Roger were still waiting to be released to their parents, when the investigation team returned to the station. After the two had been taken to seperate rooms, they recanted their story for the official report. Peter made the Teenagers vow to stay close to home, just in case they had more questions. With Mary and Roger's statements in hand, the team adjourned to the conference room.

"They came to my house, last night." Captain Stockton said to Peter as the team stepped through the door. Captain Stockton had been sitting in the immense room, waiting for them to arrive.

"Who came to your house?"

"Your Bogeymen. They almost got my wife."

"Did you actually see them?"

Captain Stockton nodded, sheeplishly. He had no desire for people to question his sanity. In spite what people thought of his mental capacity, he could not deny what had happened.

"Is she all right, Sir." Marty was genuinely concerned. Official positions aside, the Stocktons were like foster parents to Marty.

"Oh, hell yes. She's oblivious to all of this. She just thinks it was a group of hooligans come to the house to harrass me." Captain Stockton felt tears of frustration welling up in the corners of his eyes. He would be damned if he was going to sit there and blubber like a school girl in front of the troops. He stood up and fetched himself a cup of coffee.

"Captain, is she okay?" Marty rephrased the question. The urgency of her concern was revealing her emotions.

"Her sister is watching her." He said. "They came right up to the door and rang the God-damn doorbell. What kind of shit is that?"

"Captain, I know this is hard for you. But I need you to tell us everything." Peter took a roost on the edge of the conference table. He sat close enough to the Captain, so his superior would not have to strain to speak. In the last couple of days, Peter had come to think of the Captain more as a friend than a superior officer. Informality would help the Captain relax.

"What's to tell? Mar thought she heard something outside. She went to the door. I ran after her. There was six of them. One was close enough to Mar, when I closed the door, his hand was actuall stuck in the door."

"I don't understand. You trapped one of them?"

"No. I was sitting on the floor with my back against the door. I looked up, and one of them had reached his hand through the crack in the door. When he pulled his hand out, the doorbell began ringing."

Peter quickly related the reports from the Teenagers. The Captain, who had been conditioned all of his life to be skeptical, was not. For a moment, no one uttered a sound.

"So." Clark was the first to break the silence. "It doesn't appear that we're dealing with humans. Any idea what we are dealing with?"

"Ghosts." Captain Stockton said without hesitation. "Dark Ghosts."

"I think we need to seriously consider the Yurok legend of the Umais, the Tricksters." Marty said.

"What if..." Peter was lost in thought, again. He tapped his pen against his lips. "We, as a whole, are so egotistical. We believe that all life forms on this planet are carbon-based. What if that wasn't the case? Imagine what a creature would be like, if it was nitrogen-based or oxygen-based. They could be tangible, but not tangible. They could be seen, but not seen. Liquid nitrogen and liquid oxygen turns everything it touches to ice."

"I think you're onto something, Sir." Marty jumped in. "While oxygen, by itself, isn't flammable, it feeds the flame. And liquid oxygen is very flammable."

"Carbon-based life forms require oxygen to live." Peter continued. "Wouldn't it stand to reason that an oxygen-based life form would require carbon to survive?"

"So all those piles of dust out on the Jetty were, in actuality, freeze-dried body ash of the victims." Marty exclaimed.

"Clark. Why didn't you have any specimen bags?" Peter said, accusingly.

Clark shrugged, defensively. "Who knew we were going to find remains that would fit in a Zip-loc Baggie. I can only assure you that this is Marty's fault."

Captain Stockton tapped Clark on the arm. "I failed Biology. Is this making any sense to you?"

"Yeah, no. Don't worry, Sir. I got all 'A's in Biology and this still doesn't make any sense."

She was not at all what Peter had pictured in his mind. Though he hated to think that he was capable of stereotyping, he was trained to create profiles. Darla Lovesyou did not fit the profile Peter made up for her. He was expecting a hundred year old lady, with braided, long, straight, black hair. He had pictured her wearing a leather skirt, mocassins, beads, and bear claws, and carrying an assortment of rattles.

He was embarrassed. She was in her early thirties, with wispy hair light enough to be considered auburn. And, of course, she wore a T-shirt, Jeans, and Nikes, which in his defense, were made of leather.

Darla came into the conference room with the poise and dignity that one would expect from Royalty or a beauty pageant contestant. In this case, it would not have been too much of a stretch. She was beautiful, in deed.

Darla barely acknowledge the men in the room. She walked straight towards Marty, shook her hand, and sat in the chair closest to Marty. Her back was straight, and her chin was up.

"Jeez, what's up her..."

"Clark!" Peter snapped, cautiously.

Darla focused her attention on Peter. Another misconcept, she had pale, blue eyes. Peter felt as if she was reading his soul with those eyes.

"I had a dream last night." She spoke. "I was walking in the woods. It was dark. I was alone, yet I was surrounded. It was the Umai."

"If you don't want to talk about it, we'll understand." Peter quipped. Clark chuckled.

"You have a serious problem on your hand." Darla continued, undaunted. "The Umai has existed since before the beginning of time. The Judeo-Christian religions refer it to the war in heaven. They keep a low profile. They keep their numbers low. They feed on the wicked and the outcast. You have a band of Umai that are breaking all the rules."

"Why?" Peter asked.

"I don't know. World domination? Armegeddon? What you have to remember is the Umai are evil. What you have here is evil within evil. This is an elite group of evil."

"Great." Clark said. "What do we do about it?"

"How should I know? Isn't that your job?"

"Thanks. Thank you. No, really. You've been a lot of help."

"I do have a message for you. Your wife has been watching you. She likes what she sees."

If this was a joke, Peter thought to himself, it was a bad one. "Did my wife have anything to say?"

"Your ex-wife is still alive. However, she does want you to grow up. Get on with your life."

"Darla, do you have any more information for us?" Marty interceded.

"No. If you need me, I'll be home. I will do everything within my power to assist you spiritually. But your real strength will have to come from within."

Mary was exhausted when they returned home. Her parents opted to save all chastising, until she was rested. Normally, she would have rather had the punishment dealt out immediately, but under the circumstance, sleep was best.

In harsh whispers, her parents argued downstairs to keep from waking her. "Change of plans." She sat up in her bed. She couldn't sleep as long as there was a riff between her mom and dad, especially when it was her fault that they were arguing.

"I just want to know how my daughter could be so irresponsible." Her father spatted. Since she was no longer in her room, they gave up the pretense of restraint.

"Honey, that is not fair. Those children would have still gone out there, whether Mary was there or not. Let's be happy she's safe."

"I don't give a rat's ass about those damn kids. She betrayed our trust, and we almost lost her."

Mary's mother turned to her. "Your father's right, darling."

Mary sat at the dining room table. Her eyes were cast down. Times like these it was better to be invisible.

"This kid that they found with her. In their underwear, for crying out loud. Mary. Mary. Did he try putting his hands on you?"

So much for being invisible. She was wishing she stayed in bed. "He tried, Daddy. But you taught mom and me how to take care of ourselves. It's okay."

"It's not okay. He put my daughter in jeopardy. Someone's going to pay."

"Daddy, please don't do anything. I made him pay for it already."

"It will be all right, honey. Why don't you go get some sleep." Her mother interceded.

"I can't sleep if you are fighting."

"It's over, now. Right, Dear?"

Her father walked over to the table and kissed her on the forehead. "Go get some rest. You're grounded until you are thirty."

She could live with that.

15

"It's been hours since any of us have gotten any sleep, and I haven't had anything to eat in days." Clark looked down at the box of day-old doughnuts. "Anything that could be considered real food, anyway."

"Sir?" Marty had a feeling she knew where this was heading, but she figured it would be better to let it play out.

"Don't call me Sir. It's too depressing. Pete loves to be called Sir. He makes a fuss about it, but he really likes it."

"Yes, Sir. I'll bet he does."

"I'm going to go get something to eat. I was wondering if you want to come along. I'm buying."

Marty wondered how close this was to sexual harassment. The laws were always changing. Besides, she was famished. "What did you have in mind?"

"I was thinking maybe Seafood. I understand you have some great Seafood restaurants, up here."

"I guess we do. I don't really care for Seafood, though."

"What are you doing in Crescent City, if you don't like Seafood?"

"I live here."

"Oh. So what are you hungry for?"

"Pizza. I love Pizza. In fact, I know a couple of places where they would put anchovies and clams on it, if you want."

"Eww. No."

"It's Seafood."

"No, no. That's okay. There is a limit to this desire. So, Pizza then?"

"Sure."

"Hey, Pete. I mean, Sir." Clark gave a glance towards Marty. She smiled.

"What? What are you up to?"

"Nothing. We're going for Pizza. Do you want to come along?"

"Could you bring me back something?"

"Sure. Can I borrow a Fifty?"

Peter glared at Clark. Marty let a moan escape her throat. "Keep the receipt." Peter said, as he pulled out his wallet and handed Clark a hundred dollar bill.

"Clark."

"Yeah, what is it?"

"Don't call me Sir."

Marty laughed. It was the first time the two detectives had heard her laugh. Peter thought it was a beautiful laugh, almost melodious.

The pizza was half eaten, and Clark was working on his third beer. He was bristling on the inside. He tried to tell her what was on his mind, but he choked at every attempt. If he was going to get through this, he would have to take a less direct approach.

"What do you think Darla meant earlier?"

"I think she meant that deep down inside, deep, deep, terribly deep down inside, you're a nice person."

"Ha-ha. That's a good one."

"I think she meant that if your wife were alive today, she would be impressed with you."

"I've been content to live with her memories for so long. I haven't thought about anyone else. Until I met you."

Marty was speechless. She picked up her drink and nervously took a sip. After she sat the glass down, she folded her hands on the polished Formica, in hopes that he wouldn't notice her hands shaking.

"I know I've been an ass. I know I might be coming on too strong, for the moment. But one thing I have learned from the death of my wife is that life is too short. The real disaster of living is all of the lost opportunities we allow ourselves. In a minute or so, you're going to tell me that I'm way out of line, or you're going to tell me that for one reason or another I'm just not your type. Or you're going to take a chance with me. I can't miss the opportunity to find out. We'll be finished with the case soon, and I'll be back in Eureka regretting the rest of my life, if I didn't at least give you the chance to turn me down flat."

Marty took another sip of her drink. She waited for Clark to continue his monologue. Apparently, he was finished.

"Mister, I've seen through you're shell. I've seen your sensitive side and your sense of humor. I know you're a good person. I could never turn you down flat. But there is something you should know. I haven't dated since high school. I've buried myself in my career. Until recently, I've never had any romantic notions towards anybody. But I find myself having those feelings for someone else. I know you don't want to hear this, but I really want to be your friend. I know it sounds like an old cliche, but I really want to get to know you as a friend. Please tell me we can be friends."

"Yeah, of course we can always be friends."

"And mean it."

"Sure. You know, it's kind of funny. You made me forget my wife if only for a moment. But I really do still love her. And that's okay. I'm going to be all right."

When she looked at him then, Marty could sense the sadness inside him. But she knew, and she knew that he knew, she wasn't the one that could take that sadness away. Somehow, she didn't know how, things really were going to be all right. She let out a sigh.

Peter sat at the enormous, conference table. He missed his own desk. Eureka wasn't so far away. Would it bc so awful, if he left Clark here for the rest of the day? If he left at that moment, he could check his messages at the office, go home and watch TV for a couple of hours, and still be back before dark. Peter was feeling hollow inside, alone. He needed some sense of security.

He had scanned through the files again. They were on the right track. He knew this with all of his heart. What he didn't know was where they were going to go next with this case.

Peter was wishing that he had taken Clark's invitation, but he knew it was given contradictorily. He didn't want to admit that he was jealous of his best friend. His friend deserved some happiness in his life. And yet...

The conference door opened, just a crack at first, and then Darla was standing there. Apparently, she had gone home and changed. She was wearing a black sundress and heels. Her hair was different, but Peter wasn't sure how. She was wearing make-up, now. The changes made her look ten years younger than before.

"I was hoping someone was still here." She said.

"The others will be back in a little while. Is there something I can do for you?" Peter was pondering the changes in her appearance. She was certainly attractive before, but now she was even prettier. Peter wasn't one to get hung up on physical appearances, but she definitely caught his attention.

"I just feel I need to discuss the Umai with you." She walked over to Peter and sat on the table. She chose a spot that was dangerously close. "I wanted to make it clear that every Native American Nation has it's legend of the Trickster. You know him as the Devil. The Shoshone children play a game at night, called shoulder-tapping. It's similar to tag. The Shoshones name for the Umai is Hickshuwa, the Shoulder-Tapper. When you are alone at night, and someone taps you on the shoulder, don't turn around. They'll steal your soul."

"What would happen if someone were to shine a bright light on these Umai?"

"They would disappear."

"Would the bright light kill them?"

"No, they vanish with the darkness. It's like the darkness tows them away, almost at the speed of light or at the speed of darkness, as the case may be."

"What if they were completely surrounded, and a light was shined on all sides, would this kill them."

"I don't know. It's never been done before. If I had to take a guess, I would have to say no. They would escape with the darkness. Wherever the darkness goes, they would follow."

"So you don't think they can die?"

"I have never heard of any being killed."

Peter briefly related the events in the Teenagers' report from the Jetty. Then he added his and Marty's theory. When he finished, he sat and waited for Darla to respond.

"This is interesting. Generally, a person takes a religious stand, or they take a scientific stand. I have never heard of a superstitious scientist."

"But if these Umai are real, then there must be a scientific explanation. There must be a way to destroy them."

"You battle them your way, and I will do everything within my power. If you are successful, you will have to let me know. If I don't hear from you, I will know your theory was wrong."

"Have you ever seen an Umai?"

"I have not. I don't believe I would be standing here, now, if I have."

"Darla, I've got to ask you something. You have all this information. Why didn't you come forward sooner, before the Miles' boy was taken?"

"Think real hard. If I had come up to you six days ago and told you what you have learned in the last twenty-four hours, what do you think your reaction would have been? The only reason you are listening to me now is because the Umai are affecting you, personally."

"Darla, I would have listened."

"You say you would. Let me ask you one little question."

"Go ahead."

"Do you believe in the Oman?"

"The who?"

"The Oman, Sasquatch, Bigfoot."

"No! Of course not. This is hardly the ... Oh, I see what you mean."

"I have to leave you now. You're about to get some important news."

"You don't want to stay for pizza. They should be back any moment now."

"Thank you, no. And you won't have any time to eat, either. I'm sorry."

Peter looked at her quizzically. "I've gone without food before."

"I'm sorry for what I said about your ex-wife. It wasn't your fault."

"I know."

"Bad times are coming, but it's only bad for those that are left behind. Remember, those that are taken goes to a better place. Remember that and you will be okay."

There was a knock at the door. A uniformed officer stepped in to the conference room. "Detective Swann. I'm sorry to disturb you, Sir. They need you down at the beach. A body has washed up on shore."

Peter looked up at Darla. She leveled her pale blue eyes upon him. She had known, and he was sure he didn't want to know how she knew."

"Will I be seeing you, again?"

"Why can't men ask the questions that they really want to ask?"

"I don't understand."

"If you think about the question that you want to ask me, you'll know the answer to the question you did ask."

Peter thought for a moment. She seemed pleasant enough, but at that moment he felt very uncomfortable. She had control of the conversation. Peter never liked being powerless.

"Are we compatable?"

"Very good. And the answer is?" She prodded.

"No. No, I won't be seeing you again."

Darla hopped off the table. She stood close enough that her thigh pressed against his arm. When she placed her hand on his shoulder, Peter looked up into her eyes. "I just need to say 'thank you' for last night." She said.

"I don't understand."

"You don't need to understand. But thank you just the same." Peter could've swore Darla was blushing. "You better be going." She said, and then added in a stage whisper, "Dead bodies don't get fresher."

Peter watched her walk out of the conference door and close the door behind her. He jumped up and chased after her, but when he pulled the door open, the hallway was empty except for the officer who had delivered the message. "Where did she go?"

"I'm sorry, Sir, but where did who go?"

In the little one-bedroom house out on the birch tract, Darla laid naked in the center of the white circle. Her clothes had been neatly folded and placed on top of her shoes. These had been placed just outside of the circle, within easy reach.

She had never attempted to have a vision during daylight. It seemed foolish to even try. But she had so much that she wanted to say, and after she had seen him in the flesh, she felt the need to reach out and touch him. Her heart told her to bond with him.

She was the grand-daughter to the great medicine woman, but she was not the great medicine woman. Ego aside, she knew she could not handle the Umai alone, nor did she want to. He had a mighty warrior spirit within him. He was the one who could do battle against the evil spirits.

When her spirit had returned home, she was bathed in her own perspiration. She clawed at the fabric of the carpet.

Nipples erect, and thighs pressed together. She patiently awaited for the orgasms to subside, so she could breathe again. She had learned years ago not to fight the orgasmic onslaught that accompanied a large percentage of her visions. To fight against the lust-throes only prolonged and intensified the effects.

When her breathing was less labored, she attempted to get up and dress, but she found that she was too weak. The couch was within arms reach away, and the sheet was still there. Once she had the sheet in her hand and had made sure the white ash circle was unscathed, she covered her nakedness and fell into dreamless sleep.

It didn't take long to get to the beach. In a town as small as Crescent City, anywhere a person needed to go was practically walking distance, providing they didn't need to get there in a hurry. Driving was essential only because everyone in this nation was brainwashed into thinking so.

Peter made his way down the rocks and logs that separated the beach from the parking area. His gym shoes filled with sand as he made his way to where the police officers and the medical examiner were standing. Before he reached the body, he knew what the cause of death was. The young man's legs had become tangled in the kelp that grew in abundance in this part of Crescent City. The rising tide had dragged the boy under. It was a miracle that the other teenagers hadn't drowned along with their friend.

16

"The Heroine was called into the secret headquarters. As the world's greatest female espionage agent, she was called in to headquarters quite often. She was in top form, having recuperated from her last assignment. Damn, I'm good."

Mary was scribbling her thoughts down on a scratch pad, when Detective Swann, Detective Williams, and Officer Martinez came in to the conference room. Mary could tell by the grave look on their faces and their almost reverent demeanor that they had bad news.

"Mary, we need to talk." Marty said. "We wanted you to hear this from us."

"What is it?"

"A search team found the body of your friend T-Jack. His body washed up on shore, earlier today. According to the Medical Examiner's report, his legs became entangled in seaweed. The waves dragged his body under, and he drowned."

Mary had already presumed that T-Jack was dead. Somehow, hearing it now made everything so official. She squeezed her eyes shut and tried not to let the tears escape. When that failed, the sobs followed.

Peter handed Mary a tissue. Marty put her arms around Mary's shoulder. Instinctively, Mary buried her face in the crook of Marty's neck.

When Mary had finally regained her composure, she sat back down in her chair and looked up at Marty. "You have to ask me more questions, don't you?"

"Yes. How did you know?" Marty asked.

"I've seen it in the movies and on TV. Anytime you go to the police station, they need to ask more questions."

Marty smiled. She smiled on the outside. On the inside, she was smirking at herself. She was expecting an explanation of a more supernatural nature.

The two Detectives remained silent. They sat in chairs at the large table. Apparently they were taking mental notes. Mary found the whole situation very unnerving.

One of the reporters at the local newspaper had caught on to most of what had been happening and leaked the story out to the public. The stories had been so fantastic that it seemed like they belonged in the tabloids, instead of a real newspaper. The people, who have not been affected by the disappearances, laughed at the stories. Those who have lost loved ones were bitter toward the carelessness of the loose-lipped reporter. The newspaper was suffering its lowest sale and largest cancellation, since it came into circulation. Mary resented being privy to how accurate the paper was. Oblivion could be a sweet thing, indeed.

The man Officer Martinez referred to as Peter spoke. "Mary, if you're feeling up to it, we would like you to tell us everything that happened last night."

It took Mary about an hour to recap her former statement. The Detectives interrupted occasionally to ask if she might be mistaken on certain details. She was not. When she had finished recanting, there was a moment of awkward silence.

"So, what's going on?" She finally steeled up the courage to ask.

They looked at each other. Peter spoke again. "Well, Mary, we're not certain. All evidence seems to point toward an old Native American legend that someone may be trying to recreate, or..."

"Go ahead, Pete, tell the young lady your theory." The Detective known as Clark said.

"How are your grades in Biology?" Peter Continued.

"I get by." Mary confessed demurely.

"Good. I want you to hear me out. Promise me you won't think I'm crazy until you've had the chance to hear the whole story."

"Okay."

"The Indians have a legend about a group of people that only come out at night. They are referred to as Indian Devils, or ...Marty, what is the other name?"

"The Umai, Sir." Marty replied. Peter gave Marty a sideways glance of frustration. "Peter, Sir." Marty added.

"Right. Anyway, these Umais roam the night looking for souls to steal. The way I see it, if these people exist, why do they have to be carbon-based? What if they were oxygen-based?"

"Oxygen is flammable." Mary exclaimed.

"Well, actually it isn't. For the sake of argument, let's say an oxygen-based life form is."

"That would explain why they couldn't follow us into the water." Mary was trying her best to keep up with Peter's thoughts.

"How is that?"

"If they were oxygen-based, and water is two atoms of hydrogen and one atom of oxygen, then the hydrogen in the water would break them into pieces when it diffused the oxygen."

"Now, see. That never occurred to me." Peter was genuinely impressed. However, Clark just yawned and rolled his eyes. It was hard to tell if Marty was paying attention, but she was busy writing on her notepad. Mary assumed that Marty was writing down everything she said.

Mary's father, Colonel Jack Westing (Retired) or the Golden Thunder as he was known to his troops, waited until Mary's mother had gone to the grocery store. When he was sure that she was not going to double back for some forgotten item, he went to the gun cabinet and pulled out his Remington 760 Game Master. He ran his hand along the smooth wooden stock. With his right hand, he grabbed the checker grooved pistol grip. Holding the rifle as if it was a torch, he picked up his cleaning kit and can of oil and headed off for the study.

Once he had positioned himself behind his desk and laid down newspaper to protect the wood grain of the desktop, he disassembled the Game Master. He took great care to inspect each piece for rust and built-up carbon. Once he was satisfied that the gun was thoroughly cleaned, he poured a small amount of oil on a rag and coated each piece with a thin film.

When that chore had been accomplished, he went to work on the barrel. After stoking the barrel several times, he held the barrel up to the light and peered through it like a telescope. He followed the riflings from one end of the barrel to the other. When he was certain that the barrel was clean and well lubed, he reassembled the rifle.

Grabbing the magazine, he loaded it to capacity with four 30-06 rounds. One round would do the trick, but he did not want to leave anything to chance. Wrapping the Game Master in a small blanket and cradling it in his arms like a newborn baby, he carried it out into the garage and laid it on the back seat of his Ford Bronco.

There was an evil in this town. This evil came dangerously close to his family. He was the sole person to eliminate this evil. He would do his job.

Peter was impressed with this brilliant young lady. After all that she had learned, she remained sharp and unnerved. Peter was certain that the average teenager would have gone to pieces, at this point.

"Mary, we've kept you too long. May I give you a lift home?"

"Yes, Please."

As they stood up to make their way to the parking lot, they were intercepted by a uniformed officer. "Detective Swann?" The Police Officer was short of breath. "We have a problem. There are several groups of people at the beaches. They're posing as Sun-watchers, but the Captain says that this has all the ear-markings of a mob."

"Don't they know there's a curfew in effect? Marty, there is a curfew in effect, isn't there?" Peter said. Marty nodded her head.

"Well, it should be okay. We still have..." Peter glanced at the clock on the wall and then at his wristwatch, for confirmation. "Geez! When did it get to be so late?"

"Sir, Peter." Marty stammered.

"Sir Peter!" Clark laughed.

"Bear with me. It's a hard habit for me to break." Marty was flustered.

"You were saying?" Peter wanted to get beyond the awkward moment.

"There's three key locations for watching the Sunset." Marty continued, in spite of Clark's ribbing. She hurried over to a county map, that was tacked to the wall. "The prime location is here. The Locals call it 'Pecker's Knob', don't ask."

"I'll take that one, Sir Peter." Clark laughed. He stood up and put on his jacket.

"I'm warning you, Clark. Leave it alone."

"Leave what alone, Sir Peter?" Marty wished she was dead. Clark noticed how red her face had become. "Marty, you do realize that I'm teasing Pete, not you. Right?"

"No. The second place is over here. It's a little hard to get to. It's past the Airport. Once you reach the parking lot, you will have to follow a trail to the beach."

"I guess I've got that one." Peter said. "How do I get to the airport?"

"I know the way. I can show you." Mary was anxious to be a part of all of this.

Peter looked over at Marty and Clark. They shrugged. He did not like taking a civilian, but he had a feeling he wasn't going to have a choice in the matter.

"And I'll take this area, here." Marty pointed to a bluff that overlooked the ocean.

"Remember, they haven't broken any laws yet. It's for their own safety that we get them off the streets." Peter said.

"Should we clap our hands and shout 'break'?"

"Would that make you happy?" Peter said to Clark.

"Yeah, just once."

"Okay." Peter and Clark clapped their hands and shouted "Break". Marty and Mary refrained.

Marty handed her keys to Clark. "You take my car. I'll get a cruiser."

He took the keys then called out to Peter. "Hey, really. Be careful, Sir Peter."

"Leave it alone, Clark." Peter shook his head in disgust as he walked down the hallway. Mary stayed closed behind him.

Mary's father, Jack, had heard the hubbub going around town, about how a bunch of people were going to gather together and hunt down whoever were responsible for the kidnappings. If they could capture any of these costumed freaks, they would make the creep tell them where the missing persons were. If they couldn't capture any of these freaks alive, well, that was okay too.

Of course, if the locals did apprehend any of these freaky perpetrators, he would be more than happy to lend his expertise in the interrogation. But he was hunting an evil of a different kind. He sat in the Bronco, at the corner of a cul-de-sac and waited. He was prepared to wait as long as necessary. Thankfully, the wait wasn't long.

At the end of the street, a man and his teen-age son exited their house and climbed into a yellow Toyota Celica. The yellow car, an '81 GT Liftback, approached Jack's Bronco, then it turned right at the intersection and drove away. He waited until the car was a block away, before he began tailing it.

Once the Celica reached the 101, it turned south. Ten minutes later, it turned off the highway and headed for the Crescent City Overlook, a.k.a. Pecker's Knob. Jack Westing smiled. Little yellow cars were easy to follow. Once they reached the small park, which was precariously perched on a cliff two hundred feet above the ocean, the Celica pulled over to the side of the road. The parking area, designed to accommodate up to fifteen cars, was filled beyond capacity.

Jack pulled in behind the Celica. Inconspicuously, he climbed out of the bronco and followed the man and the teen-age boy. He moved with purpose, never eyeing the two. If they noticed him, they would have believed that he was a stranger with the same purpose as their own. So the three of them climbed the hill, together, or so it would seem.

The observation platform was packed with people. Those who arrived late filled the trail and parking area. Some of the people resorted to standing on the picnic tables, but the majestic redwoods that lined the park's grounds, obscured any view of the setting sun.

Jack waited until the father and son were separated. Once he worked his way through the crowd and was standing beside the boy, he scanned the group of people. When he was sure that no one was paying attention to him, he clapped the boy on the shoulder.

"Hey, aren't you Roger?"

"Yeah." Roger replied, suspiciously.

"Hey kid. I've got a plan to catch these freaks. Would you like to help?"

"What'cha got in mind?"

"I think I know where these freaks are hiding out. I just need you to help me flush them out."

"Dude, I don't know."

"Hey, kid. You want to be a hero, don't you?"

"Yeah, sure. Doesn't everybody? Just let me tell my dad where I'm going."

"We don't have time. The sun is going to be setting in a few minutes. Don't worry, your dad will be proud of you, when he sees how responsible you are."

"Hey, yeah. Good idea. Okay, Dude. What do we do?"

"Follow me."

Jack led the kid back to the Celica and the Bronco. He pulled his rifle out of the back seat, disrobing it of the blanket that had kept it concealed. With great pride, he held it up for Roger to get a good look at it, then slipped the sling over his shoulder.

"Dude. Maybe I should have a gun?"

The retired Colonel was set back at the notion, but only for a moment. "Do you have a gun?" He asked.

"No, sir."

"I see. Well okay, I think I have something you could use."

He opened the back of the Bronco and pulled out a cargo box. After rummaging through the box, he pulled out a smaller wooden box. Opening the little box, he pulled out a starter pistol. With accessories, the starter pistol doubled as a flare gun. Without the Accessories, the starter pistol looked real.

Mary's father flipped out the cylinder and dramatically made a show of loading it with blanks. His ploy worked. Roger believed he was being handed a real gun. He slipped the pistol in the waistband of his jeans.

"Careful, kid. You don't want to shoot your dick off."

Roger looked down at what he was wearing. He looked at the pistol, and then at Jack. "Where should I carry it?"

"In your hand. Make sure the safety is on. I don't want you accidentally shooting me."

"No sir. Don't worry. I won't."

Mary's father led Roger back up the hill. There was a trail on the other side of the parking lot that stitched the treeline and cliff and eventually led its travelers to the shoreline. The Sun was setting. It would be dark soon. Jack knew that there was not enough time to get completely out of ear shot, yet he needed to get far enough away to buy himself time.

"It's not too far, now. Take the safety off of your pistol, but remember, keep it pointed either at the trees or out toward the ocean."

"Okay." Roger thoroughly believed he was carrying a real gun. There was no reason to be suspicious of a man who would let him carry a loaded weapon.

"Roger, I need you to walk ahead of me. Don't worry. I've got you covered." Jack patted the butt of the Game Master, which he had cradled in his left arm since they had reached the trail.

"Cool, Dude. Keep me covered." Roger made his way across a section of the trail that had been eroded away by seasonal mudslides. Two hundred feet below were rocks waiting to smash his body, if he lost his footing. Roger sighed in relief, when he made it to the other side.

Only slightly disappointed that Mother Nature hadn't saved him the work, Jack executed the mudslide more proficiently than the kid. Roger waited until Jack had reached the other side. "Okay, kid. Take off. I'll be right behind you."

The Sun had sat, and the trail was cutting back into the forest and the darkness, therein. Soon, Jack's vision would be hampered so severely that it would prove to be ineffective. The time to act was now. He raised the butt of the Game Master to his shoulder and drew a bead at center mass.

A thought occurred to Roger. "Hey, wait a minute. I know who you are." Roger turned to face the man behind him. For the first time since the man approached him, he knew real fear. The man was pointing his rifle squarely at him. "You're Mary's..."

The hills reverberated as the impact of the 30-06 round drove Roger off his feet and onto his back. The bullet had entered high on the right side of Roger's chest. When Jack reached the kid, shock was already setting in. The kid's face was pale. Blood was gurgling from the open chest wound.

Jack was not certain that the kid realized he had been shot. But then the kid raised his pistol and fired it directly at Jack. When Roger saw that the guy that had shot him was unscathed, he fired two more shots. Again, Mary's father just stood there. Roger looked at the muzzle of the gun and back at Jack.

"Monster." Roger wheezed. Blood spurted out the corner of his mouth and across the right side of his face. Roger coughed, and more blood poured out. He dropped his hand that held the gun. His head lolled back.

Jack Westing considered putting another bullet in the kid's head. There had already been enough gunfire to draw attention their way. The kid would be dead soon.

He bent down and grabbed the kid's wrist. After he checked the trail behind him and found no one there, he dragged the kid into the thick underbrush. Pulling a pocketknife out of his pocket, he began digging into the topsoil.

He made a point of not digging too deep. All too often, when people try to conceal a murder, they make the mistake of digging so deep that they break through the topsoil, and then they don't dig deep enough to hide the scent from wild animals. Jack knew that the acidic soil would decompose all traces of the body within a week or two. Bugs, slugs, and larger animals would assist with the bigger pieces.

There was a pulse in the kid's wrist, still, but it was barely detectable. Jack rolled the body into the shallow trench. When that was done, he filled the hole, and then he used the knife to cut limbs off the surrounding trees. He covered the bare earth with a pile of vegetation.

Back on the empty trail, he fired the remaining shots of his Remington 760 Game Master at random trees. Jack half expected the kid to dig himself up and come bounding out of the underbrush. Nothing happened. The kid was dead.

Jack had his story already in his head. He only hoped he would sound convincing enough. There was always the possibility that people would not believe that he was shooting at shadows. Shadows that picked up a teen-age boy and packed the kid into the woods.

17

Darla Lovesyou sat on her heels. She was well within the center of her circle. The Sun was setting, and her little living room was growing dark. This would be the night that her magic would be needed the most.

She thought of lighting more candles, but she had already started her incantations. There was no time. This was the night that evil would make its stand. All humanity would lose if she made any mistakes.

She should have been alone, but the tapping on her shoulder told her differently. At first, she tried to ignore the Shoulder-Tapper. Curiosity got the best of her. She had to know how it had gotten inside her circle.

She spun around and fell on her butt. Standing outside the circle, with his toes not quite touching the circle, was an Umai. He was holding a broomstick. Darla could see frost collecting on the wooden handle.

"You are ruining everything." The Umai spoke in a deep, raspy voice.

"You cannot win." Darla mustered up the courage to answer. She broke out in a cold sweat that covered her bare skin.

The Umai tapped the tip of the broom handle on the floor by the circle. With the broom handle, he began scratching at the white ash. It wouldn't take much to desecrate enough of the circle, for him to step inside.

Darla looked around for the bag of white ash. She had left it outside the circle and out of reach. If she stepped out of the circle, he would have her. If he got inside the circle, he would have her. She looked around at the circle. It was over for her, but maybe she could still turn the tides in humanity's favor. She reached out to one of the corners of her circle and grabbed an amulet that laid closest to 'Fire'.

She thought of Peter's face and whispered a prayer. If she had time, she would have grabbed an amulet from each of the corners and said a prayer for each of the warriors. Peter's face was still etched in her mind when everything became dark and cold. Very, very cold.

Marty was trying ineffectively to disperse the crowd at Brother Jonathan Park when a car scream to a stop. The driver rolled down his window and yelled that some kid had just been abducted at the Overlook. Like rats abandoning a sinking ship, people scurried for their vehicles.

Marty grabbed her hand-held CB. "Clark do you copy?"

"Marty?" Clark's voice came back over the airwave. "I'm kind of in the middle of something."

"What's going on?"

"Mahem. Pure Mahem."

"I'm on my way."

Peter's voice emitted from her hand-held. "Marty. I didn't copy Clark's end. What's up?"

"Apparently, some kid was abducted. Everything is chaos. I'm on my way up there."

"Call the station and get backup." Peter continued. "We'll be right behind you."

"On my way. Out." She placed the call to the station and turned on the siren. It was good to know that some people still had respect for the law, as they pulled their cars over to the side of the road to let her pass.

A few minutes later, she reached the S-curve of the 101. She had reached the straightway when she noticed a single, shadowy figure standing just out of the light of a streetlamp. "That doesn't seem right." She said to herself.

"Clark." Marty spoke into the microphone. "You've got backup on their way. I'm going to check on something."

"Marty. I've got to tell you. Now would not be a good time to go off on your own."

"Marty out." she answered.

"Marty! Marty! Peter do you copy? Peter?"

Marty swung the cruiser around. She pulled the car over where she had seen the dark figure, but the person was gone. She climbed out and glanced around. The figure was a few blocks away, walking down an unlighted street.

"How could he have gotten so far, so fast." She said, in amazement. By the time she got back in the car and drove to the new spot, the person was gone again. Without getting out of the car, she spotted the dark figure walking around a strip mall that housed a cinema and the Safeway grocery store, two blocks away.

Several seconds later, she parked the cruiser in a box-shaped alley. she grabbed her flashlight and climbed out of the car. As best as she could surmise, she was alone. Unholstering her revolver, she approached a dumpster. There was enough light emitting from the security lamps that she could see, without the aid of her flashlight.

"Have you found what you were looking for?" A voice came from behind her.

She spun around. Despite the lights that shined indirectly from the roof of the strip mall, Marty could not make out any features of the man that stood between her and her cruiser. He seemed to emit darkness. More importantly, he had her boxed in.

"Hold it right there!" She said, as she brought her service revolver up at arm's length and pointed it at the dark figure.

"Oh please." The man said. He took two steps forward.

"Sir! Stop right there." She said with more determination. Without taking her eyes off of the man, she depressed the button on her hand-held.

"This is Martinez requesting backup." She spoke into the mike, trying to keep the edge of urgency out of her voice.

Clark's voice came over the receiver. "What's going on, Marty?"

"Clark. Oh thank God. I'm trapped."

"Where are you?"

"I'm behind the Safeway strip mall, by the cinemas. One of the suspects have me blocked off from my vehicle."

"Sit tight. I'll be there in five minutes."

Peter's voice crackled with static. "Clark. I'm on my way. I should be there right behind you."

"Copy that." Clark's voice responded.

The shadowy figure took three more steps. His movements were casual and unrushed. He seemed unafraid, almost as if he was enjoying the suspense.

"Sir. If you take one more step, I will be forced to shoot you. Now, please. Put your hands behind your head and kneal on the ground." The man took another step. "Sir. Did you hear what I said? Kneal down or I will shoot you."

The man took another step. Marty couldn't be sure, but she thought the man was chuckling. She grabbed the revolver with both hands, aimed at the man's chest and slowly squeezed the trigger. When the revolver bucked in her hands, the dark figure stood, unwavered. The driver's side window exploded into hundreds of pieces of fragmented glass.

The man took another step. Marty still could not make out any features in the man's face. It was as if she was staring at a shadow. Her mind went blank, as she emptied her revolver into what should have been the man's mid-section.

He took another step. Marty flipped the cylinder out. She reached in her jacket pocket for a speed-loader. Her hands were trembling as she tried to reload her weapon. Her heart leaped in her chest, when the speed-loader slipped from her fingers and fell to the pavement with a metallic thud.

This time, the man took three quick steps, so he was standing directly in front of Marty. He placed a hand on her shoulder. The coldness of his grip bit through her jacket, her shirt, her skin, right down to the bone. The revolver fell from her hand.

"Oh my God! No!" She screamed. Her head lagged away from the man. She fell to her knees, but the man's grip remained. Her left arm became useless, as his icy talons dug in. She clawed at the pavement with her free hand, trying to find a hold that she could pull herself away with.

"Please! Oh God! Please." She could feel her body being lifted towards the darkness. The freezing pain was replaced with numbness, fear, and the inevitable. Her eyes could no longer focus, so she closed them and waited for the end.

"Get away from her!" Clark's voice slammed through the darkness.

Marty opened her eyes, and though everything was fuzzy, she made out Clark's image running toward them. At the speed that Clark was charging, he meant to tackle the dark figure. Instead of hitting solid matter though, Clark fell into the dark form. Marty saw the look of surprise in Clark's face, before he vanished.

The dark figure released his grip. His body bucked, as he and Clark became one entity. Red dust fell in a large pile at the dark man's feet. Marty closed her eyes.

Time passed. How much time, Marty could not be certain. She knealt there waiting to die, waiting for the darkness to overtake her.

"Marty?" It was Peter.

"Over here!"

Peter was running toward her. His weapon was drawn. She recognized fear in his face.

"He's got Clark." She looked around. She was alone. Tears escaped the corners of her eyes.

"Where are they?" Peter stopped running. He continued to move toward her, walking hesitantly.

Marty said nothing. She looked down at the pile of red dust. It all seemed so surreal.

Peter walked over to the pile and squatted down. His back was toward Marty. He was close enough that she could have reached out and touch him. He said nothing.

Slowly, he reached out and grabbed a fistful of the freeze-dried remains of his partner. He pulled a Zip-loc bag out of his pocket and place the contents of his hand into the bag. He filled the bag with his best friend's body ash. Marty wished he would say something. Anything.

"We need to get you to the hospital." He finally spoke when he saw her shoulder.

"We don't have time. We have to go after them."

"How?"

"I have an idea." Mary was there. Marty was not aware of when Mary had arrived.

"No." Peter said. "We have to get her to the hospital."

"I'm fine, for now."

"We go to the Jetty." Mary continued. "We can trap them on the Jetty."

"This is crazy!" Peter said.

"Listen to her, Peter." Marty laid her good hand on his forearm.

"How do you know they will follow us?"

"They can't afford not to." Mary said. "We know too much about them. But we have to go, now."

Peter wrapped his arms around Marty and helped her to her feet. She winced when pressure was applied to her left side. Peter kept his arms around her, until she was situated in the gold-colored Cimmeron.

"Okay, now what do we do, Boss?" Peter said as he climbed in behind the steering wheel.

"We need a couple of cans of gasoline." Mary said. "We're going to set the Jetty to blaze."

18

Mahem reached city-level. The word spread quickly of the young man's apprehension, right in front of a retired Colonel. According to the gossip, the poor man fired four shots into one of the creatures, but they were able to drag the kid off, all the same. The retired Colonel was taking it pretty hard. He blamed himself for not doing a better job of protecting the kid.

Jenna Harding, mother of three, realized too late the inevitability of life. She had attended the sunset party at the Front Street Park. When she heard the news about the teenager being taken, it all became very real to her. She thought of her own children at home. People were panicking all around her. Some were even carrying guns. She was wise enough to know not to hang around with a panicking mob with guns.

She wasn't running around, like the others. People were crashing into her on their way to nowhere. No one noticed the three men standing just outside the light. Three men who stood and watched the chaos unravel. No one noticed except for Jenna.

Mr. George Parker, the balding, heavyset owner of the Parker's Drugstore, plowed into Jenna. They both tumbled to the ground. Mr. Parker jumbed to his feet with a spryness that could only be explained by the adrenaline coursing through his blood stream. "Bitch!" He spatted at Jenna, then took off on his haphazard route without a thought of assisting Jenna to her feet.

Once she was up again, she made her way to the well-manicured lawn of the soccer field. She was free from the maddening crowd, away from the cars, away from the lights. Instinct caused her to look over her shoulder.

She spotted the three men. It appeared that they had noticed her as well. Their footsteps matched her own. She picked up her pace, until she broke out into a sprint. Unlike the mass of hysteria she had escaped, Jenna ran with a purpose. Her children were waiting for her, at home.

When she reached Front Street on the other side of the park, she stopped to look back. There was no sign of the mysterious men, yet fear was still heavily upon her. She ran past the post office, a bank, and a few shops. Finally reaching the corner of 4th and H street, she paused to catch her breath.

Jenna's ribs felt as though they were piercing her lungs. The left side of her abdomen was cramping. Tried as she might, she couldn't keep from doubling over. The metallic taste in her mouth told her that she was out of shape, and she was pushing herself too hard. She still had six blocks to go, before she reached her house. She had to press on. It never registered in her head that she was standing on a sewer grating.

An ethereal octopus arm slipped through the metal grating and wrapped its grasp around Jenna's ankle. The pain in her leg was so quick. She assumed it was from so much running after all these years of sediment living. To her surprise, when she attempted to run again, she fell flat on her stomach. She sat up and looked back at the grating. Her right leg had broken off just below the knee and was frozen to the sewer cover.

"Oh my God! No!" She screamed.

The grating flew up in the air. A black blob wooshed out of the hole. It landed on Jenna, completely covering the mother of three.

Peter was grateful to find a gas station on the north end of town that was pushing the curfew back. He sent Mary in to have the attendant fill three five-gallon gas cans. He instructed her to tell the attendant that this was a police emergency. Setting the flashing dome on the roof, Pcter hoped the attendant would realized the authenticity of the situation. After he placed the flashing red light on the roof, he retrieved a first aid kit from the trunk.

With the assistance of the Cadillac's inner dome light and the flourescent lights of the convience station, Peter had a good view of Marty's shoulder. The leather material of her jacket crumbled away, where the Umai had grabbed her. Below the jacket, her shirt broke up into a coarse powder. Peter could see her flesh, now. It was a bluish-gray color. He grabbed a pen and prodded the exposed skin. it was solid like a frozen pot roast. Marty had not reacted to his examination, so he looked up at her face and found that she was studying him with her eyes.

"How bad is it?"

"We need to get you to the hospital."

"This first. We do this first."

"Does it hurt? Are you in pain?"

"Only when I try to move it."

Peter covered the affected area with a couple of dry, sterile 4x4 pads. He took a couple of cravats, and with the first cravat, he made a sling for her arm. Marty winced, as he assisted her arm into the sling. Peter used the second cravat to wrap around her body and anchor her defunct left arm from swinging or being jarred.

"Sir Peter." Marty giggled. "Sir Peter, I've got to tell you something before it's too late." She paused for Peter to respond. Peter didn't say anything."

"Clark told me that he was attracted to me."

"I know. What did you say to him?"

"I told him that he was a good person, and that I thought of him as a close, personal friend. It's not easy for me to have friends, but I do consider him a friend. I hope he realized it wasn't a brush off."

"But..."

"But I told him I was attracted to someone else."

Peter felt hot tears welling in his eyes. No emotions, not yet, he told himself. Darla's words came back to him. He tried to imagine Clark, dressed in white. In Peter's mind, Clark was walking through the proverbial Pearly Gates to his wife, who had been waiting for him all these years.

"It's you, Sir Peter." Marty said. She was still studying him with her eyes.

"We need to get you to the hospital. You're delirious."

"Why would you say that?"

"I'll ask you if you remember what you said, when this is all over."

"I won't forget."

Mary came back to the car. She was being escorted by the store attendant. The attendant walked around to the driver's side of the Cadillac.

Peter was sure that Marty wasn't going to remember any of this, if either of them lived to remember this moment at all. He was just about to tell her that he had feelings for her also, when the attendant rapped on the window. Peter flipped back the toggle switch that lowered the electric window.

"I'm sorry to bother you, but this is highly irregular." The gas station attendant said. Peter sensed that the guy in the funny vest wasn't really sorry. "We have policies about filling gas cans, you know."

"This is a police emergency!" Peter could feel the blood vessels swelling in his temples.

"I'm sorry, Sir. I'm going to have to see proof." Once again, the kid wasn't really sorry. Peter suspected that the kid has had a few run-ins with the law, and this was his way of getting his revenge.

"Did you happen to notice the red light that is flashing in your eyes?"

"Well yeah, but that doesn't prove anything."

Peter had uncharacteristically lost his patience. He unclipped his shield from his belt. Then he pulled out his service revolver and stuck it in the cocky attendant's ribs. The expression on the attendant's face was one of a person who was about to spill his bladder.

"Do you realize that you are violating a Curfew, and that I could have this place closed down?" It had taken Peter a lifetime to achieve his trade-mark stoic composure. This punk was ruining it.

"I w-was ju-just getting ready to close up sh-shop."

"I could run you in to the station and make you sit in a cell until I got around to feeling like questioning you. I'm kind of busy right now, so you would probably be sitting there for a while. So, do you feel like cooperating, now?"

"Yes Sir. I'm sorry, Sir." The boy jumped back.

"Don't call him 'Sir'. He hates that. It's Sir Peter to you." Marty's words were beginning to slur.

Peter closed his eyes and rubbed his temples. When did it all go so bad? He wondered.

The gas station attendant ran over and grabbed three gas cans. Once he had them in his arms, and he was certain he wasn't going to drop them, he ran over to the pumps. Under Mary's supervision, he proceeded to fill the cans.

"Hey!" Marty tried to grab Peter's sleeve, but she could not reach, and moving caused a great deal of pain. "What if he didn't accept the gun as proof?"

Peter shook his head. "I probably would have shot a couple of his toes off."

Marty laughed. Laughing caused pain to shoot from her shoulder into her chest. She winced and grabbed her arm. "Don't make me laugh. It hurts when I laugh."

"I'm sorry."

"That's okay. You only hurt the ones you love." Marty held the expression on her face, as if she was waiting for a confirmation.

Peter didn't know how to react. A deep chuckle escaped his chest. He knew what he wanted to say, but the timing seem all wrong.

Mary climbed into the back seat, with the three gas cans. The attendant came back to Peter's window. Peter was getting real tired of seeing this young man's face. He rolled the window down.

"That will be $45.75."

"You can't bill the Police Department?"

"No, Sir. $45.75."

Peter pulled out his billfold and handed the attendant a one hundred dollar bill. The attendant looked as though Peter had handed him a snake. He started to walk away then tried to hand the bill back to Peter.

"I can't change this." The attendant was as annoyed as Peter.

"Keep it." Peter said, forcing a smile on his face. He turned the engine over and put the Cadillac in drive. Once they were back on the 101, he pointed the car in the direction of the Jetty.

"You gave that guy a hundred?" Marty said.

"It's only money."

"Ooh yeah, baby. You and I? We're definitely dating." Marty giggled.

"One more word out of you, and I'm turning this car around to the hospital."

"I'm fine."

"I'm thinking about a psych eval."

Marty giggled again. Mary leaned over the seat. She was genuinely concerned. "She's not fine. What's wrong with her?"

"I'm not certain. It could be shock or delirium. It might just be her endorphins kicking in. One way or another, we'll have to keep close to her." Peter picked up the mike. "Dispatch? This is Detective Swann. Do you copy?"

"Dispatch copies." The raspy voice on the scanner said.

"Dispatch, can you connect me to the Coast Guards?"

"Hold one."

19

Ensign Lovett was sitting at the com, when the Detective's call came through. He copied all of the instructions down, so he could pass the information on to the Officer on Duty. The instructions, though quite bizarre, were simple enough. He sounded the alarm and spun around in his chair to face the door. The Captain would be coming around any moment.

Five minutes passed. The blue-gray steel door remained closed. Ensign Lovett scanned over the instructions that he had written down on the yellow legal pad. If the message hadn't been routed through the Police Department, he would have suspected a hoax.

Another five minutes passed. He wondered if the Captain was stuck in the head. If the Captain was in the middle of a nature call, surely someone else would come to receive the report.

It had been fifteen minutes since the alarm was sounded, and the door remained closed. This was most peculiar. The clamor of the alarm bell was giving the Ensign a headache. Finally, he stood up and headed for the door. "If Muhammad won't come to the mountain, let the peon track down the Chief and hope they don't shoot the messenger. Or something like that."

When he slipped through the doorway, he noticed a small heap of red dirt. He kicked through it with the toe of his patent leather low-quarters. "I'm not cleaning this up." He said aloud.

Once he reached the Captain's Quarters, he knocked on the door. There was no reply. He knocked again. When no answer came, he opened the door, a crack. Cautiously, he opened the door, a little further. When that warranted no response, he opened the door enough to poke his head in. The Captain's Quarters was deserted. The door to the Head was standing open. It was plain to see that the prestigious Captain was not taking a dump.

Ensign Lovett looked down at the yellow notepad. All he wanted to do was hand the assignment off to someone, anyone at this point. He ran down the narrow, blue-gray corridor to the Sleeping Quarters.

He stepped through the door and found himself alone. This did not surprise him. No one could possibly sleep with the alarm going off. At least now, he knew where the pile of red dirt had come from. There were several piles of it on the floor. A few of the beds were covered in the red dirt. The Captain was going to freak when he saw that.

Since the Captain's Quarters was empty, and so was the Sleeping Quarters, Ensign Lovett surmised that the crew was already aboard the ship and probably waiting on him. Twenty minutes had passed since he sounded the alarm. If the crew was on the ship, waiting for him, they were going to be mad. It was not his fault. He knew it was not his fault.

To get to the ship, Ensign Lovett had to run through the Dining Facility. It briefly registered that there were more piles of the red dirt on the floor, chairs and tables. It was bothersome, which a room famous for being clean enough that one could eat off its floor, had become so dirty. Heads were going to roll, one of which was probably his.

Picking up his pace, he made his way out to the docks. The Jedediah, a "Manitou" class medium Harbor Tug with two water cannons installed at the aft, was still anchored and tethered to the dock. There was no sign of life on the Jedediah. He was alone.

The thought occurred to him to radio The Coast Guards in Brookings, Oregon and pass the assignment off to them, at least until he solved this mystery. They could reach the Jetty from the north side in a little over twenty minutes. Providing they kept their nose to the sonar, they could avoid the rocks and get close enough to the Jetty to use their water cannons.

As the Ensign stood there contemplating his next move, he felt a cold chill travel up his spine. What started as a cold breeze, turned to pain, and then numbness. His yellow legal pad fell from his fingers, tumbled to the deck, and then slipped off into the water. Someone distinctly tapped him on the shoulder. When Ensign Lovett turned to see who was behind him, he was enveloped in blackness.

Across the harbor, The Coast Guards were scrambling to launch their firefighting tug. Peter had gotten the message to them that a Police Detective and two others were going to light the breakwater on fire. The Coast Guards were to use their water cannons to knock anyone off the breakwater that would try to stop them.

With the wall of fire and the water cannons, they could not lose. The Umais would be trapped on the Jetty. If the Umais did not catch on fire, The water cannons would sweep them into the ocean.

Peter popped the trunk open. Mary grabbed three road flares and tucked them under her belt. Next, she loaded the flare gun. She kept the flare gun in her right hand.

Peter opened Marty's door. She just sat there staring out the windshield. Peter squatted down beside her.

"Marty? Marty. We have to go now."

"Oh, Peter. I don't feel well." She slowly turned her head so she could see him. The pain in her shoulder traveled up her neck.

He caressed her cheek and brushed her hair back from her forehead. She was cold and clammy. Peter could tell by her sluggish movements that her neck had become stiff. He was angry with himself for not taking her to the hospital. She would have been safe in a well-lit hospital, with an armed guard sitting in her room.

"Please, Peter. Leave me here. I can cover your rear from here."

The idea of leaving her behind was out of the question. "I can't. I can't leave you. You wouldn't be safe here, by yourself."

"Have Mary stay here with me." She pleaded.

"I hate to say this, but if I left both of you here, why would they want to follow me?"

Slowly, Marty tried to turn her body. Peter assisted her in standing. Once she was on her on accord, Peter grabbed a gas can in each hand and headed for the trail that led to the Jetty. Mary handed the flare gun to Marty's one good hand, so she could use both hands to carry the last gas can.

Peter sat his cans down, long enough to help Marty execute the gate. He was trying to keep an eye out for any sign of the Umai, yet he honestly didn't know what to look for. The Lighthouse's beacon was wreaking havoc with his night vision. The foghorn wailed balefully. A fogbank was making its way toward land. It was coming from the northwest, pushing a cold front ahead of it.

To make Mary's plan work, They would have to have water on both sides of the Jetty. Since the tide was on its way in, they had to hike about a half mile to get to a spot that would suffice. Marty was walking aimlessly and came dangerously close to the edge a couple of times. She sobbed, softly. It was truly different from the tough, headstrong Police Officer Peter met, just a few days before.

Peter sat one can down. Keeping the second can, he began retracing his tracks toward the shore. When he had counted fifteen paces, he uncapped the can and began pouring its contents onto the deck of the Jetty. He poured in a serpentine fashion, until he reached the first can.

He sat the empty can down and picked up the first one. The three of them walked together for a short distance. Marty leaned against Peter, as he kept a protective arm around her. It made his heart ache to see her so helpless, but there was not anything that he could do about it. If they survived this ordeal, there would be time to heal, and mourn the lose of his best friend. For now he had to be strong and keep his wits about him.

Once they had walked another fifteen paces, they stopped. Again, Peter retraced his steps to where he left the empty can. He emptied the other can in the same manner as the first.

Marty stayed with Mary, as Mary dumped her can of gas the way that Peter had dumped his. She had to keep pausing to see where Marty was, gently guiding her away from the edges and away from the volatile puddle. It was a slow process, but since she did not have to backtrack, she had emptied her can before Peter.

When Peter's can was empty, he straightened up to see how the girls were doing. Marty was oblivious of her surroundings, But Mary was shouting something to him. She was too far away, and the ocean breeze was too strong, for him to make out what she was trying to tell him. She pointed frantically at something behind him. He turned to look at what she was pointing at. What he saw made him freeze in his tracks.

Six dark figures were standing abreast, like a scene from the OK Corral. Peter wished he had thought to leave a marker at that end of the Jetty, so he could tell when they had stepped into the area of the gasoline. It was probably better this way. There was no point of alerting them, if they weren't already.

Peter's heart was racing. They were real. This was not some frantic person's hallucination. This was not a dream.

When Peter had spotted them, they weren't moving. They just stood there as if they were trying to calculate his next move. Slowly, they began to advance. They didn't move in unison, like marching soldiers. Instead, they staggered their advancing line, like team players or a mob hell-bent on keeping their opponents from crossing over.

Peter stole a glance back at the girls. Mary had finished emptying her can of gasoline. She had an arm around Marty's waist, as they walked backwards away from Peter. Mary was keeping her eyes trained on the Shadow People just beyond Peter. Though Mary and Marty were so far away from him, he could tell that Mary was terrified.

When he turned his attention back to the Umai, he was unnerved to see how much distance they had covered in such a short time. There was no doubt about it now. The Umais were standing within range. He pulled a flare stick from his own belt. Once it was lit, he held it high above his head, like a marathon runner for the Olympic Games.

"Let the games begin!" He shouted, not really caring whether he was heard or not. Hunkering to the ground, he touched the flare to the puddle of gasoline.

The Umais were running toward him at an incredible speed. The puddle of gas made a whooshing sound as it took off on a foot race of its own. Two Umais on each side managed to leap over the sides of the Jetty, into the relative safety of darkness. The two that were in the center were not as lucky. When the wall of flames touched them, they burst into fireballs. Peter could detect the smell of ozone in the air.

There was a surreal cold gush of air that washed over Peter, from behind. When he spun around, he found that no more than five feet away stood the remaining four Umais. By diving into the darkness, they could travel at a tremendous speed. One Umai stepped forward.

"Leave him to me. He's mine." The shadow man snarled in a deep raspy voice. "Go get the other two."

"Okay. I give up. You've got me trapped." Peter said. He raised his hands above his head. He still held the flare in his right hand.

"Drop the fire stick. Resistance is futile." The Umai's voice was deep and sinister.

"Come closer. Let me see your face." Peter said.

"Drop the fire stick." The Umai said more firmly.

"You're right. You're right. I'm beat." Peter sighed. His shoulders slumped as he brought his arms down. He tossed the flare toward the feet of the Umai and into the puddle of gasoline from the second can.

"Noooo." The Umai yelled just before he caught on fire.

Peter watched through the ever-growing flames. The remaining three Umais realized the situation. They began running, almost flying, toward the women. Their speed was so great that they easily stayed ahead of the wall of flames that pursued them.

Mary watched the Umais charging in her direction. Peter thought she was too scared to move, but then he realized that she was calculating the Umais' distance. She raised the flare gun and fired it at the deck in front of the ghostly stampede. The flare skipped along the Jetty, igniting the volatile puddle as it danced about.

Again, two of the Umais escaped by diving into the darkness. The third Umai caught ablaze, as the two walls of fire met.

This time, Peter really was trapped. He was safe in his ring of fire, yet he was powerless to help the women.

20

"The handsome hero was trapped behind a lake of fire. The Devil's cold-blooded henchmen, literally cold-blooded, crept closer and closer to the young and beautiful heroine and her wounded friend. If they were going to survive, it would be up to the heroine to seize the moment. Damn, I'm good."

Mary tucked her fingers of her left hand under Marty's belt. she had already cast the flare gun away and replaced it with a lit flare stick, in her right hand. Slowly, the two remaining Umais advanced toward them. When the Umais reappeared from the darkness, they appeared between Mary and Marty and the lake of fire. Had they reappeared behind her, she would have been trapped between them and the fire. For each step that the Umais took toward the women, Mary echoed their movements and took a step back. She gently tugged at Marty's belt, and Marty followed.

Mary wanted to run for the maze, but the maze was still a half mile away. Marty was in no shape to run, and Mary couldn't leave her behind. Besides, Mary doubt if she would have gotten far, before the Umais were upon her.

Mary glanced to her right. If the situation became helpless, Mary would give Marty a shove and hope that Marty cleared the rocks and tetrapods below. True, Marty was in no condition to be swimming, but she would be safe a little while longer. It would have to be on the harbor side. If they went in on the ocean side, the waves would dash them against the breakwater. Even at ebbtide, the waves were crashing impressively.

Without advertising her intent, Mary slowly guided Marty closer to the harbor side of the Jetty. With each step they took, they drew nearer to the edge. The Umais had somehow shorten the distance between themselves and the women. They seemed to be feeding off of Mary's fear. Mary swung the flare, like a sword, in a long, wide arc.

Something was wrong. They could have rushed her, yet they seemed to be leading the women, or herding them. Mary spun around. She had made a mistake. She miscounted. The third Umai was standing close to Marty. He was almost close enough to reach out and touch Marty.

Instinct took over. Mary lunged at the third Umai. She stabbed forward with the lit end of the flare. The flare buried into the chest of the Umai. When he exploded, Mary was standing so close that the emitting flames licked and bit at her bare skin, singeing her hair.

Marty mumbled incoherently. Mary whipped Marty around the burning pile that had once been an Umai. Mary spun around again, still holding the lit flare in her hand. The remaining two Umais were charging, but they stopped in their tracks, when she turned to face them. They had no features to their faces, yet Mary could hear them softly chuckling to themselves. She knew what the source of their amusement was. She only had one flare left. It wouldn't last til dawn. All they had to do was kick back, relax, and wait.

If Marty was feeling better, Mary could use the last flare to push the Umais back toward the lake of fire. Marty was not getting better. She was becoming weaker. Mary couldn't risk going over the side, and she knew that she would never make it through the maze, not with Marty in tow, not in the dark.

Mary and Marty were trapped.

Jerot was old. He had watched the rise and fall of great men, of new nations, of empires. He had seen the eruptions of volcanoes, such as Mt. St. Helens and Pompeii. He had witnessed wars such as World War II, World War I, Masada, and Troy.

When the Gods sent two meteors crashing through the watery atmosphere, and the waters poured out of the heavens above, he and a small band escaped the Great Diluge. They had learned of Utnaphistim's plan to build a ship. Jerot and his team stood watch as Utnaphistim filled the ship with many animals and large bins of food and storage. One night, a week before the meteors, they moved into the ship, under the cover of darkness.

During the days that the ship floated aimlessly, they refrained from assimilating humans. The man, who was later known as Noah, and his family were saved so that there would be food for the Umais in the future. Instead, the small band of Umais were forced to subsist on dumber beasts. They had to be systematic to avoid detection.

The lizard birds were the first to become extinct on the ship. Due to the lizard birds' foul smell and bitter temperment, Utnaphistim and his sons never realized that the lizard birds had disappeared. The same held true for the raptors. Jerot remembered the night they assimilated the raptors. The creatures were so ferocious that assimilating them had given Jerot an orgasmic rush.

Three days before the ship settled on land, the small band of Umais assimilated the one-horned horses. There were so many horse-like animals, Jerot was certain that the horned ones wouldn't be missed. He was wrong.

When the ship finally settled on Arafat, and all the animals were set free, Jerot and his followers remained in the darkness. The humans left the ship to set up tents on dry land. Utnaphistim was never certain if it was a relief of cabin fever, or if it was that eerie feeling that they weren't alone, but he and his family were eager to abandon the ship.

One night, when Utnaphistim had drank himself into a stupor, his wife returned to the ship with morbid curiosity. she ventured into the darkest bowels of the ship. Using old rags and discarded tethers, the Umais trapped and gagged her. When she had been properly bound, they lit upon her. Each Umai assimilated a small section, keeping the woman alive for hours, until everyone had partaken of her nutrients.

Morning came. His wife was gone. Utnaphistim speculated that his wife had left him to mate with one of the beasts in the wilderness. He vowed that her name would never be uttered or recorded.

When Jerot, the old one, came up with the plan to take back the land and even the score with the humans, it wasn't hard to find Umais to follow him. True, they would have to violate some Umai laws. In the end, the humans would bow down to them. After all this time, the humans would realize their role as Umai fodder.

The plan was a simple one. They would find a community that was low in population and easy to cut off from the rest of the world. They would make their presence known. After the chaos had subsided, and all the key figures had been subdued and assimilated, the humans would realize the futility of their existance. From that small community, they would be able to branch out, ever widening their reign.

Everything had gone wrong. He had underestimated the collected abilities of five humans. The holy woman, three warriors, and a young girl had all but completely annihilated his team. He was certain that by eliminating the holy woman and one of the warriors, the others would become more docile. Even with another warrior, the cop lady, mortally wounded, the remaining two had fought admirably. They were a cunning breed.

After assimilating the holy woman, his original target had become the female warrior. He settled for the Detective that came to her rescue. Had he stuck to the original plan, or had he took the time to assimilate both the Detective and the female

Police Officer, the situation would be different. Even though she was not assisting the other two, she was not much of a hinderance. The remaining two had still killed four of his followers.

Now, the young woman had them at a standoff of sorts. If he pulled back, the enemy would be stronger. If he eliminated the Detective and the young woman, the town would be theirs. Even though his numbers were down to two, including himself, if he did away with this threat, more Umais would join him.

He would win. The Detective had trapped himself between two lakes of fire. The girl refused to sacrifice her friend to save herself. She was limited on her ammunition. All Jerot had to do was wait. Oh yes, he would win.

21

Peter sympathized with baked potatoes, as he slowly roasted. Though there was plenty of room between the two lakes of fire to keep his clothes from catching on fire, the heat was intense. He could not stay there much longer.

He tried to see how Mary and Marty were doing through the forked tongues of the flames. He could just barely make out Marty's and Mary's shape through the waves of heat. The Umais were invisible to him. He had seen a fireball beyond where the girls had been standing at the time. If that was an Umai burning, there were only two left of the six. He prayed that there were only six.

Gasoline is very volatile. The liquid burns off much quicker than oil or diesel. The flames had already subsided to waist level. However, Peter knew he had to get back into the fray if Marty and Mary were going to survive.

Peter stared out across the harbor. The Coast Guards should have been there. They could have had the fire out already. Their water cannons could have dispersed the Umais easily enough. Nothing was moving on the harbor. No lights were flashing. No one was coming.

He thought of the gurus who walks on red hot coals and decided that he did not have enough faith for that. If he jumped off the Jetty on the harbor side, he would have to swim at least a quarter mile, in hypothermic waters, against a waxing tide. All of this was providing that he did not break his leg or neck in the process. The ocean side of the Jetty was even worse. The waves would definitely smash his broken corpse against the breakwater. And yet...

He ran to the ocean side of the Jetty and sat down on the edge. He felt nothing against his feet except the wall. The fire had hampered his night vision, and the sweeping of the lighthouse's beacon was aimed too high to penetrate the darkness below him. Nine feet below him, and about seven feet out, he could barely make out the white foam, as the waves swished through the cavities in the rocks and tetrapods.

He rolled over onto his stomach. He still felt nothing. Scooting down until he was resting on his elbows, he found a couple of toeholds on the wall. By repositioning his hands, he was able to lower himself down to the rocks. The rock that his feet came to rest on had a sharp edge that jutted upward. Peter needed the wall to help keep his balance. A wave hitting the wall below him, sent a spray up between the rock and the wall. After his experience in the broiler, the spray felt good. Just the same, he was grateful he was not swimming in it.

As he inched his way along the jagged edge, his eyes slowly became accustomed to the dark. He was able to make out black shapes of rocks against the blue-black night sky. The jagged rock came to an end. He stretched out his leg and found a foothold on the next large rock. Testing his weight to make sure he was not going to fall, he leaned toward the rock and felt around the surface until he found a crevice to slip his fingers into.

He worked his way around the boulder by first finding a place for his hand, and then a place to put his foot and so on until he reached the other side. Once he had made it around the boulder, he found a pile of rocks that led up to the deck of the Jetty. The waves were coming in with more force. The tide was definitely coming in. As he scrambled to get to the top of the wall, he found a driftwood stick. The wood was damp from the Ocean's spray, but Peter had a feeling it would come in handy.

Once he reached the top of the rockpile, he realized that he had not gone far enough. He was not going to be able to continue this route, either. It had taken him too long to come this far.

The flames had waned to about eighteen inches. Peter could see through the licks of flames. There was fear on Mary's face. He still could not see the Umais. Judging from the way Mary kept diverting her attention from side to side, they must have been planning to rush Mary from both sides.

Marty was not looking well. It wasn't the lighting. Her Complexion was an ash-gray color compared to Mary's. If these shadow bastards didn't get a hold of her and reduce her to a pile of red dust, like Clark before her, she would succumb to shock and die anyway.

Peter laid one end of the stick in the fire. He thought out what he was about to do. Somehow, he wasn't afraid. If he was successful, Marty would be safe. Whether he lived or died was irrelevant. When he was sure that the stick was lit enough that it would not sputter out at the wrong time, he pulled it out of the fire. Looking at the flames, He paused for a moment.

"Go ahead, Hero. Save the world. Save the fair maiden." Peter knew he was alone. The voice came from inside his head. It sounded familiar and took him a second to realize that it was Darla Lovesyou's voice inside his brain. After this was all over he would have to look her up and tell her to knock off all of this American Indian voodoo shit.

"Don't worry. The fire won't hurt you." The voice continued. Holding the stick in his right hand, he did a tuck and roll right into the lake of fire and came up running. He could tell by the heat and sizzling sound that the back of his jacket was on fire.

As Peter ran to Mary and Marty, he could make out the Umai that stood between the women and himself. his pant legs were on fire, all the way up to his knees. the heat on his feet, lower legs, and back was intense. It was stifling his breathing. He kept his legs moving. As long as he was still running, Mary and Marty still had a chance. He didn't care if he made it or not, as long as he took at least one of the remaining two Umais with him.

Peter cleared the fire lake and was still at a full run. He could tell by the light reflecting off the moisture on the Jetty's deck that he must have resembled a fireball, himself. He wasn't sure if he was breathing or not. He hoped he wasn't. A lungful of smoke, gas fumes, and even flames would be bad at a time like this. Just a little further and he would be on top of his unsuspecting target.

Out in his peripheral vision, he saw the second Umai, who up to this point had been invisible to him. The second Umai had realized Peter's intentions and was charging to intercept him. Peter kept to his original target, but the second Umai was faster than he. When Peter was within six feet of the first Umai, the second Umai flew up in the air, as if it had sprouted wings, and landed on Peter's back. Peter's burning jacket instantly ignited the Umai. There was a deafening woosh and a percussion that threw Peter face first, on to the deck of the Jetty. A wind, that was simultaneously hot and cold, swept over him. He was unaware that the gust of air had snuffed out the flames that would have killed him, otherwise. He rolled over, hoping there was enough sea water on the deck to put out the flames that were, fortunately, already out.

When he stood up, Mary, Marty, and the last Umai were gone. The lake of fire was just a few sporadic flames. The other Umai was still burning, those flames were dwindling. The air was heavy with the smell of ozone.

Peter spun around, sweeping the area with his eyes. Had he lost? Did the last Umai overtake the women?

"Mary! Marty!" He shouted.

"Peter!" Mary's voice was faint and distant. She tried to run for the maze, towing Marty along, while Peter was distracted. Once again, she was at a stand off.

Peter ran along the Jetty. Amazingly, he was unsinged by the fire. There was a lot to be said for the power of faith, he thought to himself. He stopped running when he was able to make out the form of the Umai.

Mary and Marty were trapped. If Mary tried to run, The Umai would overtake her. Mary had lit the last flare.

Peter drew his service revolver and fired three rounds into the Umai's center mass. The shots were ineffective, as Peter knew they would be. The Umai turned to face Peter. Since he had failed to grab his burning stick, Peter was virtually unarmed. Mary's flare would be burned out in minutes. It was over. They had lost.

Peter fell to his knees. "Mary, take Marty. Jump into the Ocean. It's your only chance." He thought those words more than he had actually spoke them, but he hoped Mary had gotten the message, just the same.

Suddenly, Peter felt a tap on his shoulder and a strong, cold breeze on his back. When he looked up, he saw three more shadow people pass by him. Two converged on the last Umai, and took hold of him. The third dark figure positioned himself in front of Peter.

"No! You can't do this! Join me, and we will succeed!" The remaining Umai screamed, but the two had a strong grip on him.

As they dragged the last Umai past Peter, Peter felt another cold gust of air pass over him. He also felt another sharp rap on his shoulder. This time, Peter kept his eyes focussed on the one standing in front of him.

"You are Detective Peter Swann. You are a Polie Detective, specialized in tracking down missing persons. You reside in Eureka, California. Stand up."

"I'm afraid you have me at a disadvantage." Peter slowly stood up and faced the one addressing him. "You know me, but I don't know you."

"We have existed on this earth almost as long as your kind have. Our presence has been kept from almost all of your population. What you know now, you must forget. You must not speak of this to anyone."

"What if I do?"

"We know you, Peter Swann. You are in our minds' eye. You cannot escape us."

"Every day, I get reports of missing people. I have a file cabinet full of unsolved cases. How can I stop this? How can I stop you?"

The dark figure leaned in close. Peter caught an overpowering scent of ozone. "You are not here to control us. We are here to control you." The dark figure snarled. After the Umai visibly recomposed himself, he added, "There was a murder of a young man, tonight. The young girl's father did it and is blaming my people." The dark figure produced a folded piece of paper, seemingly from nowhere, and handed it to Peter. It was too dark to see what the paper was, so Peter tucked it in his pocket.

The shadowy man walked past him. Peter turned around. "Why are you telling me this?"

"To protect our anonymity. Besides, Chaos is our number one concern, and there will be Chaos." Having said that, the dark figure disappeared.

Peter turned around again. He ran to the women. "Are they gone?" Mary said.

"Yes. I think they are. Hold the flare up, for a moment."

Mary held the flare up. It was almost out, and she was getting ready to toss it in the Ocean. Peter pulled the piece of paper out of his pocket. It was a map of Crescent City. The paper was crumbling around the edges. In the lower left corner of the map, there was a hole in the shape of a man's fingertip. The mysterious, dark figure had put his fingerprint on the spot where Roger was buried, but his touch ate through the paper, as it did at the edges where he handled it.

"What is it?" Mary said.

"I don't know. I'll have to take it to the station to have it analyzed." Peter lied. "Come on. Let's get out of here." Peter picked Marty up in his arms and headed towards the car.

22

Everything was the same. His desk was just as he had left it, so many days ago. Nothing was moved. Everything was in order. Nothing felt right.

After he had arranged for Mary to be taken safely to her house, Captain Stockton accompanied him. They personally escorted Marty to the Emergency Room at Sutter Coast Hospital. Once Marty was in the care of the Doctor, Peter returned to the hotel room. He could not remember how long it had been since he had slept. This time, he dreamed of fighting black dragons with a flaming sword and winning.

He woke up five hours later, amazingly refreshed. After packing his own belongings, he took great care in packing Clark's clothes and toiletries. Clark had not brought a lot, so it did not take long before the car was loaded. Peter stopped at the Crescent City Police Department and ran down his report to the Duty Officer. He included his suspicion of Jack's involvement in the murder of Roger. When that was done, he climbed into his gold-colored Cimmeron and made one more stop before driving back to Eureka.

So there he sat at his desk, contemplating what it was that made him feel out of place. Why should he have to fight off the feeling that he did not belong? He was home.

There was more paperwork that needed filing. He had to be careful what he wrote. The public was not ready for the truth, and he was not ready to spend the rest of his life locked away in some psych ward.

"A group of six men, all dressed in black and armed with chemical spray guns that dispersed liquid nitrogen, terrorized the small community of Crescent City." He typed into his computer. "Several people are missing and presumed dead, including one police officer, one investigating detective, one security guard, one four-year-old boy, one Native American woman, and possibly four FBI agents. Unconfirmed accounts are still accumulating."

Peter paused. If he had not stopped by Darla Lovesyou's house to find answers to some puzzling questions, he never would have known... He wondered if anyone ever would have. How long would it have been before she was missed? How many more are missing?

"One officer was seriously injured and hospitalized with third-degree frostbite to her left shoulder, as a result of being sprayed with the liquid nitrogen." He continued to type. "Five of the six perpetrators met their demise, when they were trapped in a fire, and the liquid nitrogen in their spray guns ignited. The sixth perpetrator was swept out to sea by a wave, is missing, and presumed dead."

Peter had tried to access more information on the FBI agents, but the Bureau had closed the case to all outsiders. They tried to convince him that it was not related to any events in Crescent City. Since it would not serve his purpose to pursue the matter, he dropped the idea. It did not feel right to whitewash his report, but then again, what did these days?

Captain Jamerson stepped outside his office door. He had a stack of papers in his hands. Rather than approaching Peter directly, he stood there, watching. The Captain approached him, when Peter stopped typing and looked up at the Captain. Weighing his words carefully, Captain Jamerson placed the forms in front of Peter.

"I checked into some things. It looks like Clark named you as his beneficiary."

"He didn't have any next of kin, Sir."

"It will entitle you to a hefty sum. At least $500,000."

Peter did not care about the money. He did not know what to say. He said nothing.

"It's as if he knew he would go first." Captain Jamerson continued.

Nothing the Captain could say at that moment would make Peter feel better. "I don't understand, Sir."

"I know the two of you were close. Maybe he's sending you a message from the grave. Maybe it's time for you to get out of the game."

"I don't need the money. I'm okay, Sir."

"Damn it, Man! Take the money. Take some time off. Step away from the game for a moment. It'll be here if you want to come back. But you owe it to yourself. There's no shame in stepping out. You're finished." Captain Jamerson started to walk away, paused, and turned around. "Peter."

"Yes, Captain?"

"Don't call me Sir."

"Yes, Captain."

Peter knew the Captain was wrong. The game was just beginning. Arguing would have been pointless. He thought of his partner. The fistful of red dust had been placed in a vase and buried next to Clark's wife. It was the least that Peter could have done. He placed the overnight bags, containing Clark's clothing and toiletries, in his own closet. He was sure that they would remain there, untouched, for a long time.

He took a couple of days to close out all of Clark's affairs. There was more paperwork to contend with. After he thought about it, he conceded to take the money. Not knowing where to start, he knew he would use the money to hunt down the rest of the Umais.

There was a matter of one business still left unfinished, in Crescent City. He packed his bags, loaded them into the gold-colored Cimmeron, and drove the car north. He had called twice a day to check on her status.

When he stepped through the sliding doors of Sutter Coast Hospital, his heart leaped into his throat. Perspiration formed on every square inch of his skin. Had he made a mistake by coming? Would she welcome the sight of him? Or would she rather forget everything that has happened? He wondered.

A Nurse led him to a private room. Marty was dressed and sitting on the side of her bed. She was being discharged. The motion of Peter walking through the door caught her attention. She looked up at him. Her eyes sparkled and glistened with tears that had not quite formed into droplets.

"I thought you counted your losses and bolted."

"I promised you, I would come back and test your memory." He said. Peter hoped he appeared more confident than he felt.

"I remember everything up to driving away from the gas station."

Peter played the whole scene out in his mind. It occurred to him what she was saying. He smiled, and noticed that she was smiling also.

"I've called every day to make sure you were all right."

"I know."

"So how are you doing?"

"They had to take some skin and muscle tissue from my thigh, to repair my shoulder. It's okay. I never liked myself in a bikini, anyway." After a moment she added. "I promised them I would do my exercises, so I won't have to do physical therapy. And I have some sick leave and vacation saved up."

"So what are you waiting for? Let's get out of here."

One of the nurses insisted that Marty was to be wheeled at least as far as the lobby, in a wheelchair. Once they had reached the lobby, Marty insisted that she walked out of the hospital on her own accord. Rather than creating a scene, the Nurse consented. When the nurse walked away with the chair, Marty threw her right arm around Peter's waist. He hugged her, taking care not to jar her arm, and kissed the top of her head.

In each other's arms, they strolled through the sliding doors. Captain Stockton and his wife were walking up the sidewalk. "You were coming to give me a ride." Marty giggled nervously.

"Don't be silly, honey." Margot Stockton replied. "We were coming to see you off. You take care of yourself, now."

Marty gave them a hug. "If I don't, he will." She slipped back under Peter's arm.

It was a beautiful day. The Sun was shining. Peter could not remember if it had been sunny, before. Once they were in the gold-colored Cimmeron, Peter drove south, along the coast. For the first time in a long time, he felt like he belonged.

About the Author

Born the fourth son and fifth child of Donald and Colette's ten children, James has lived in Oregon, Washington, Utah, South Carolina, Texas, Missouri, California, and Germany. He has a degree in Nursing and currently works for a company that assists developmentally disabled adults in the activities of their daily living. He has learned to love reading from both of his parents. His father was an avid Science Fiction fan, while his mother enjoyed the Harlequin Romance books. When James was still in grade school, his older brother, Tony, would read to him from Tony's own creations. This planted the seed for James to want to be a writer, also.